ENCOUNTER
IN
PRAGUE

STORIES BY

JARDA CERVENKA

WHISTLING SHADE
PRESS

Saint Paul, MN
www.whistlingshade.com

First Edition, First Printing

April 2018

ISBN 978-0-9829335-7-2

Cover photo by Jarda Cervenka

Interior illustrations by Hannya Ani Robinson

Book and cover design by Joel Van Valin

Some stories in this collection have appeared in the following publications:

Whistling Shade - "Killing Warden Polda"

The Notre Dame Review - "Close Encounter in Prague", "For the Love of Trilobite",
"Importance of the Craze", "The Woman Who Knew 1005 Males",
"The Visit to La Casa Fitzcarraldo", "The End of the Party", "Fish and Snuff Chewing Venus"

Printed in the United States of America

Also by Jarda Cervenka:

Mal D'Afrique

Revenge of Underwater Man

Fausto's Afternoon

Celebrated Navigation: Selected Stories

To usual suspects I love:
Bohden, Henry, Jackson and Luca
great readers and fun

Stories

Close Encounter in Prague

Stan and Lida recognized their senior caricatures instantly when they met head-on promenading during the intermission. In the magnificent interiors of the Rudolfinum Concert Hall they had been walking with elevated thoughts, Telemann's music still reverberating in their chests and minds. So their meeting woke them suddenly, as if startled from a dream by one blast of a shotgun. They recognized each other after at least four decades. Both stopped speechless at first, and then pronounced their names. Lida stopped motionless as if flash-frozen by liquid nitrogen.

"Lida?"

"Stan? You in Prague?"

"Yes, yes. How many years, how many years it has been?" Stan stuttered. "Half of the twentieth century," he answered his question.

She nodded her head. "You were gone that long, Stan." Then there was nothing said for a while; they did not just look at each other, they considered themselves.

Two emigrants, exiles, he American, she Swiss, encountered their new physiognomies in the city of Prague, the place of their youthful past adventures. Some exploits had faded away, the sins of which pleasurable memories are made; some were conserved, frozen in time. Only they knew.

They walked to the bar and ordered champagne, remembering their favorite. They talked, hesitant at first, looking into each other's eyes, their thoughts not always revealed, asking conventional questions, answering them carefully, as reminiscing goes. Stan soon recognized that his memory of their common past was much inferior to the memory of Lida.

She saw him gray, with the flat eyes she knew—only now they were hooded, with appropriate sags where expected, and wrinkles, but some intelligence instantly recognizable in his mask. His memories were not concealed completely.

He observed her to be not yet fully metamorphosed—still with features he used to admire, which had not entirely disappeared over the decades. She wore her hair in a bun, now, very tidy, above a face with some hollows; wrinkles, not very deep, were shooting up around her cheeks and chin. Her evening eyes were a shallow blue-gray. When she spoke the wrinkles would be momentarily gone and she looked young again, if this could be believed. She started to dig into the past without small talk; she did not want to just chat. It was obvious—she forgot to drink, her hands agitated.

"Do you remember how we missed the train going to ski in the Krkonose?" Lida asked. "A few inches of new snow had fallen the night before, powder, and we walked to the tram station on Wenceslaus Square, and there you put on your skis, you had hickory and tonkin bamboo poles, I remember, and you skied down Wenceslaus Square—people stopped to watch you, they hadn't seen a skier on the square, ever, they applauded and cheered, and you, Stan, you waved at them only once, like a dictator, some caudillo, greeting his underlings." Lida gazed somewhere into the past, a smile on her face. "You looked serious, magnifique, I can see it clearly, now… you were superior."

"Whoa, I remember, just a little." Stan lied shamelessly, surprised to see the expression on the face of his friend.

"I fell in love with you, then." Lida whispered the announcement.

The electronic gong sounded the end of intermission, freeing them both. Hurriedly they decided to meet after the concert by the statue of Antonin Dvorak in front of the Concert Hall.

Stan was there first; he watched her descend the staircase at a very careful pace; small steps, concentrated on the stairs, betraying the fragility of her musculoskeletal state. He was surprised by his surge of sympathy.

After a few comments on the genius of the baroque masters Stan suggested a cafe in nearby Maiselova Street, in the Jewish quarter.

"Sounds good Stan, but how about my apartment in Karmelitska, where champagne cools in the fridge? Ten minutes by taxi."

❄

So soon they entered a historical building, renovated in the seventeenth century, so old that the granite thresholds were worn down concave; the stony walls of the entry hall reeked of damp centuries, and the courtyard paved with maroon cobblestones glistened as if oiled. On the top floor, behind a heavy oak door, they entered a modern, luxurious apartment. And, indeed, champagne—Bohemian Sekt, brut zero—was found cooling in the refrigerator.

Stan, himself an affluent physician from America, did not suffer any complexes, and so he praised and admired the paintings by Czech masters like Lhotak, Zrzavy and one abstract Kupka; he marveled sincerely at a cubist bronze by Gutfreund and at the big, hundreds-years-old porcelain stove of white and gold tile, in the corner. Lida was happy to guide him and to explain; it helped to cover her uneasiness, while facing the unexpected.

"I come here every year. My hubby bought it for me. I come to Prague and to this place for the music," Lida said.

Stan opened the bubbly and the celebratory decibels of the cork hitting the ceiling released some of the tension. They drank to their surprising encounter, and health, too, to satisfy conventions. The primitive sound of the cork on the ceiling lifted their mood, made their smiles natural; they were prepared to tell stories of their lives.

Both divorced only once, remarried, had a couple of children; all the kids had left their homes for distant locations. Stan became a renowned scientist and professor at a St. Louis, Missouri medical school. Lida became a secretary to a leading officer in the Women's Organization of a conservative political party in Zurich, Switzerland. Her husband was still living, a very rich man whose job and hobby was investments. After he invested early in companies prospecting and exploiting shale for oil in North Dakota, he'd doubled his millions and they moved to Lausanne, where they built their last house.

"Is your wife still alive, Stan?"

"Alive and quite well, for her age."

"And how did you meet her; you must have a story."

"Well, it is a strange story, I guess." Stan leaned back and took a sip of champagne. He liked to tell stories, but lately he experienced memory lapses which he considered ridiculous and damaging to his reminiscences. This story, though, was unaffected. "She was a scientist," he continued, "working in a similar field as me. I had never met her but one day I had to call her in California, I needed some data. We talked a lot, and I liked the tone of her voice, so I called her again few days later. We chatted about nonscientific things, and I learned she was an avid skier, like me. So I told her, I had a reservation for a week in Jackson Hole, wouldn't she like to come, too? And she was game, sure thing she said, and I promised to find a room for her, if possible in the same hotel where I was gonna stay. I failed. There was no longer even a single room available in the whole of Jackson Hole. So when I called her, she sounded so sad—so I just risked it, what could I lose, I thought, and suggested she could stay with me." Stan laughed at the memory, shook his head. "You would not guess … she said OK, I'll be there. Just like that. Maybe it was the pragmatic scientist in her, I don't know. So, I met her in person in the bed of a hotel in Jackson Hole, Wyoming."

A shadow of sadness, perhaps, on Lida's face said to the narrator that the story might not be amusing to certain listeners. But the bottle was finished, so another one came from the fridge, and Stan said it was now Lida's turn to tell a story. She was brief, describing a meeting of sponsors of her political party, where she was introduced to an interesting man, who admired the speed of her typing, and looked at her as if he liked her. A lot.

"He told me my hands and fingers were like Rubinstein's. And when I typed it sound so beautiful, like hail falling on a roof of cedar shingles. This I couldn't have forgotten, and so we met few times again and I married him in a year. I was no child bride, and it was no calf love, mind you. And he was no Romeo, either. He was somewhat elephantine even then, but it worked." She added that their marital contract worked to their mutual satisfaction, conventions fulfilled, and life was not adventurous but pleasant with him. "He was, is, a gentle man. And I have had everything I wanted," she swept the room with her hand, pointing at the painting by Kupka. "But not everything, Stan, not everything." She looked at him with flat, drooping eyes.

It was time to open the second bottle of Bohemian Sekt, this time with difficulty since Stan's hands had lost some coordination. When they toasted to meeting again in future, Stan saw her, for a second, as when she was smooth, when her glands were young, when her face was not yet crumpled silk-paper.

"You promised to take me to the Medical School ball, remember? On Shooters Island it was. And then you cancelled," Lida said. "But I went with Denny Bertold, a friend. It was a masquerade ball, but I recognized you easily, you wore only a simple mask over your eyes." Lida looked into her glass as if seeing the dance of masks, perhaps. She raised her lids slightly: "You waltzed with a tall woman who wore satin black dress with large red flowers on it. She was standing out, she was different with her mask, too. She was a bird with long sharp beak, like a saber. A beak for plucking eyes out of victims … still alive."

Stan realized it was high time to either leave or to abolish history, to step out into a different time zone. "Lida, how about we eat something!" He got up shakily, and stumbled, opened the refrigerator. But the escape was not to be.

"I cried in the bathroom there the rest of the night," Lida said, "but I forgave you, I would have forgiven you everything, then, everything. Like a bono-bono female—I was ready for anything, you know."

"I did not know that woman," Stan mumbled, "I never even saw her face under the mask. I swear!" Then he brought two pieces of cheese from the fridge and served it on the board of olive wood. "Beautiful wood, this," he said, "don't you think?" His plea for some sympathy for the wood did not seem to work. She tilted in and out a small, semi-translucent fluorite statue of Buddha on the table, forward and back again. Her sullen expression did not change.

She tried to reach for her purse, lying on the Gutfreund, but failed and knocked it off instead. Stan dropped on all fours and crawled to retrieve the bag, howling like a wolf. It did not induce amusement from his friend. She took out of the purse a billfold and from it she pulled a small square of paper. She unfolded it carefully—it was breaking in the folds—and spread it on the coffee table. On the paper, obviously an ad from a newspaper, there was a photograph of a man. They observed him in silence. Stan could see some semblance to himself in the old times. The hairline was his before it had disappeared, the lips too, and the nose—close. On each side of the nose the eyes were of a stranger, though.

"I did not have your picture, dear, but I found this photo resembling you, can't you see it? I have been carrying this for…decades. Always with me." She looked lucent, now. "He was a kitchen supplies salesman, I think, this man," she said.

Stan did not comment, he could not. He poured the last glass of champagne and with a waifish grin finished the Ementaler. Despite his precancerous state of being and general decrepitude he retained a healthy appetite, whatever happened. They both observed the picture on the coffee table, with a smile now, their thoughts unreadable.

Stan got up and crossed to sit next to Lida. He put his arm around her shoulders. With the other he caressed her hand, the veins, which resembled a mangrove tree, branches entangled, aerial roots and all. He traced the branches with his forefinger. She covered his hand with hers, breathing. He reached out to switch off the copy of a Tiffany standing lamp; it was an act of Pavlovian conditioned reflex, as if he sniffed the pheromones released from the bubbles of the bubbly. Lida sat motionless—thanatosis was the rapid diagnosis in Doctor Stan's mind.

She turned her imperturbable eyes on him. "Stan, if you are gonna undress me now, you would have to stay, you know, stay here with me."

※

Stan could not remember what happened next, he swore to the gods he could not remember a thing. Alcohol, he said; he testified that he had no idea what happened, not a clue…

For the Love of Trilobite

"... trilobites, indeed, could be considered the most important fossilized marine arthropods, essential for biostratigraphy, evolutionary biology and even plate tectonics. They first appeared 540 million years ago, in the early Cambrian, and existed for 291 million years—till their final demise in the late Permian, about 251 million years ago. But we'll come to that later..."

Marie took a deep breath, as if she wanted to shed some nervousness. Dr. Marie Podbabska, a newly appointed Assistant Professor in the Department of Paleontology, School of Geology, Charles University, Prague. She was presenting her first seminar, and it was on the topic of her scientific love—trilobites. Her main problem in designing the lecture was to eliminate the less important facts from a 45-minute presentation. After describing the anatomy of a trilobite, pointing out the uniqueness of eyes with 360-degree vision, and the extreme variation in size, from 2mm to 75cm, she paused, before stressing:

"... the incredible diversity in morphology! This makes life very difficult for a poor paleontologist. Taxonomy and phylogeny show us, amazingly, eleven trilobite orders, five thousand genera and, so far, twenty thousand species!"

At this point Dr. Robert Cerny, from the Department of Mineral Resources, thought he would leave, but, then, he liked Marie, and it would be pretty rude. After all, he thought, it was nice to look at her, sweating it out—and with some grace. He knew that grace came from knowledge of the topic; she was known for being good, in the School. And Robert, being a self-described lowlife and victim of delayed puberty, would stay just to watch her Africanized behind.

Slender, she was, but her curves were well delineated, her chest of ample quantity. Her orange-blossom honey-colored hair was pulled into a luxurious horsetail; her face was Scandinavian, oblong, with a small nose and both lips succulent; and the teeth were American, perfect. Her eyebrows, at an uphill slant, gave her a slightly worried mien, which instantly disappeared with even a suggestion of smile.

Men adore female anatomy, but it is through the face and brain they fall in love—both of which are situated above the shoulders. And Dr. Robert Cerny liked her face much—it was one reason he came to the lecture.

"The hard, dangerous work in limestone quarries was done by quarriers." She was at the conclusion of the lecture. "They lived in villages along the Berounka river and west around Prague. And these poor quarry men learned that the little creatures they saw in the stones, fragments of the stones, were of interest to Dr. Antonin Fric in the National Museum. And he might pay a few *kreuzers* for unbroken specimens. So the more curious and/or intelligent men learned that the little "crayfish" Dr. Fric called trilobites, were the most valuable of all the fossils. In time, the quarry men developed their own nomenclature for trilobites, to enable them to communicate, which, I believe, is unique in paleontology. Unique in the world."

Dr. Podbabska looked at her watch and frowned. "Not much time left," she said, "but if you'll bear with me I'll read you few quotes by Dr. Fric, as he wrote in 1863. I think it would add some dimension to our dry stratigraphy and morphology. He writes: 'Quarry men know some trilobites under Latin names, but typically use names they themselves create… During my trips around Prague I was meeting in the limestone quarries people of unusual character. After being asked if they put aside some fossils, they answered uniformly they had none.' Then Dr. Fric described the haggling about how much, how many *kreuzers* or goldens would change hands in case some fossil was, by chance, discovered somewhere. He ends, describing the end of a meeting with a rock-breaker: '"…humbly, Highborn Sir, I make no proposal and leave it on your kindly opinion. I would be happy, Sir, as you are a noble man." The quarry man parted with a low bow and repeated attempts to kiss my hand,' Dr. Fric remembered."

Marie looked at her watch. "Now … allow me to deviate further from the science … I'll show you a few slides of trilobites and tell you the names quarry men invented for them. It requires you to stretch your imagination a bit. These are from the Silurian Barrandenian formation: *Paradoxides bohemicus* was 'Spike', *Bohemoharpes bubuvicensi,* 'Horseshoe'—you can see why—*Proetus bohemicus*, 'Monkey head'—that one is good— *Koneprusia brutoni* was 'Fly with spike', and I have 40 names more." She paused.

"Sometimes I wonder," she continued, "if these semi-literate quarry men knew more paleontology than my esteemed colleagues in the Department of Mineral Resources, for instance." The speaker looked into the eyes of Robert Cerny for the first time during the presentation, and grinned.

"Well, my time is up, so thank you for your attention."

Marie hung around, hoping for somebody to approach her with a question or opinion, but everybody rushed out, with the exception of a young woman with an auburn afro, who wondered about the evolutionary connections to *limulus polyphemus*, the horseshoe crab. And then there was Dr. Robert Cerny.

"That was good, Marie, pretty good," he said and tried to shake her hand, awkwardly. She was still high, flushed a little.

"Wasn't I too nervous, you think?"

"Maybe the first minute, but then you were a real pro, I swear."

"Yeah, yeah, you say."

"But you know, the end about the quarry men and how they named trilobites, and about Fric, that was something I'll remember. And the pictures. Very cool!"

"Oh, I am glad to hear that—I thought that part might be out of place."

"On the contrary, Marie, you brought not only a piece of folklore, which, I bet, nobody in the bloody School knows about—but a little poetry into paleontology. I love that. How about coffee downstairs?"

So Turkish coffee it was; Marie calmed down and stopped combing her hair with her fingers. They watched each other's faces. They smiled a lot, talked about professors in the School, agreed on the excellence of "Saurus" Augusta and "Handsome" Pertoldi, the mediocrity of Spindlarski, and laughed at the cult of the "Big sheik," Herr Professor Kottner. Rob touched her hand and was surprised by his rising feelings of, say, sympathy. He decided to risk it.

"How about a dinner—to celebrate your talk? I don't want to be pushy, but I really would like to take you to the Cantina in Mala Strana—they have some great Mexican food."

There was a long pause before Dr. Marie Podbabska, with an ironic grin, suggested she would have to go home and change. It meant she said yes—and it was a very happy moment for Dr. Robert Cerny.

❄

In the Cantina, over flaming fajitas, their mating slow-dance began hesitantly, but the tempo increased with the help of a few mugs of twelve proof pilsner brew from Pilzen, the real stuff, accompanied by wide smiles, a couple laughs and touches.

"You know, my apartment is just a few hundred feet from here, Karmelitska Street 16, kitty-corner in front of the church of that Prague Baby Jesus. What do you say, Marie, dear?"

"What could—or should I say?" she asked, and finished the tankard of brew, now without foam.

"I have a bottle of Barrilito, there."

When Marie asked what Barrilito was, Rob knew it would happen. Excitement filled his chest as if he'd won a lottery. Men are like that.

"You'll like it, it's the best aged rum from Puerto Rico, forbidden to be used in mixed drinks, cocktails. They serve it there as you would serve an old cognac, only to a best friend."

"Am I your best friend, Rob? Or do you see me now just as a 'popular girl?'"

He took her unprotesting hand: "You are the bestest, most popular person in my book, I cross my bloody heart, and you look … bombastic …. and I like you enormously, Marie. I do."

So they walked those few hundred feet and Marie told Rob that his stratagem was primitive and totally transparent; she could see now the proximity of the Cantina to Karmelitska 16. He laughed and said nothing. Lies wouldn't do. At the apartment they had the Barrilito nightcap straight, then she threw her bra into the air; it landed on the chandelier hanging from the ceiling. Later Rob learned it was her immutable habit.

They made love of mediocre quality because Rob could not help himself from thinking how happy he was—he was flooded with feelings. Then they lay in peace, holding hands like kids, Rob thinking he would give a million bucks for a cigarette, Marie thinking she should have brought a toothbrush. She told him she had lived like a goddamned celibate nun, recently. She looked at her Timex: but still, she mused, it was only six-and-a-half hours after he'd told her she did good on the trilobites speech. That fast!

They continued their affair, fell in love with the speed of lightning and developed, in time, true friendship, too. After one year they both had thoughts about permanency—which, of course, would be the end of an interesting story. However one day…

❄

"…. I got the dough, Robert, I got the grant!" Marie danced a pirouette, then had to calm herself down—there were people around. "And it is Corsica! Remember? Looking for the *Proetus* trilobite, the last of the class before they became extinct. Remember?"

"Unbelievably great!" Rob congratulated and followed with a French kiss. They celebrated with the local bubbly Rychle Spunty (Speedy Corks), talked about Corsica, about travel money, and rejoiced in both having similar schedules in the School, lecturing in the spring semester. So they could go together.

"I asked several people in our department what comes to their mind when they hear the word 'Corsica.' One mentioned the stupid habit of vendetta, and another said the most mountainous island, next to Sardinia, and the birthplace of Napoleon. What comes to you, Rob?"

"Oh, right away I think of the French Legions. They are stationed there, in Corsica; they cannot be on French soil proper, by law. I read an autobiography of a legionnaire, just recently."

"I think I've heard of the Legion. Tell me."

"Well, in short, these warriors of *Légion Étrangère* are a legend. About half of them are not French; many escaped the law, or families, and in the Legion they could get a new identity, name. The past was forgotten, but they must swear total obedience and sign a contract for five years. They have been described as cutthroats, sundry fugitives from justice, but I think it is too harsh to call them 'scum of the earth.' You know, they become highly disciplined professional soldiers, all qualified as Commandos."

"Sound like tough guys."

"I guess they are. They are given an honorary place in the parades on the Champs-Elysees during national celebrations."

"Do you think we'll see them in Corsica? I'd like to meet some. I wonder how they look?"

"I am absolutely certain they would love to meet you, ma girl," Rob chuckled. "You can bet on it."

In the fall, when the weather in Prague grew sad, Doctors Podbabska and Cerny took a train to Livorno and from there a ferry to Ajaccio, the capital of Corsica. The ferry's progress was not a happy affair. To save money they stayed on the lower deck and when a storm hit them at about the level of Napoli everyone got sick. Marie threw up down into the Mediterranean, and people on the upper deck vomited at the heads of the proletariat on the lower deck. It was disgusting ; there were no showers available.

In Ajaccio, where they checked in at the youth hostel for twenty hard euros, they double-showered and stopped smelling like rotten eggs smashed in vinegar.

"Smell me, Dr. C!"

"A sunny field of wildflowers, Dr. P." He sniffed her like a bloodhound. All was good, again.

In the morning Marie and Rob hitchhiked south and made it all the way to Bonifacio. This was the plan the geologists agreed upon: to save up money, so as to spend it on the best seafood diners they could find, they would sleep outside under the sky, for free.

That day they had packed a couple of sandwiches, a geological hammer, a Brunton compass, and half a bottle of native wine (Vin de Corse Coteaux du Cap Corse) and were on their way, almost singing. When they came across a deserted limestone quarry a few miles northeast of Bonifacio, Marie quickly determined it was upper Carboniferous, and that there were fossils everywhere in the rubble (mostly brachiopods, some bivalves, corals, and an occasional nautilid). On the rocky wall there was a 'forest' of ivory-like crinoids, some in perfect shape, which excited Marie.

"Look, couldn't you imagine them swaying in the tidal stream hundreds millions years ago, their tentacles luring in some unfortunate arthropod. This is so cool." Marie stumbled in delight. The hunt for the big prize started. Rob found it. He was sure it was a trilobite. He constrained his excitement, picked up the rock, and since the life of true love must be nourished by small deceptions, he placed it in a way of Marie so she would be the one to find it. She picked it up shortly, remained quiet, sat on a boulder, held back the tears.

"What is it?"

"Rob, this is an almost perfect specimen, not even the pygidium is missing."

"Whoa, show!"

"This is it, this is *Proetida*. The last of my beloved class of Trilobita, before they disappeared, Robert. The last Mohican in their evolution!"

"So happy for you. That's why we came here."

"Just look at those beautiful composite eyes, like it's alive."

They opened the bottle and she sprinkled some vin ordinaire on the pale limestone ground: "Blessed be the late Carboniferous!"

Robert took the fossil from her hand, laid it on the rucksack, then stood her up and lifted her into the air, in the silence of the quarry, with no birds, crickets, or wind, the echo of their voices just imagined. The collectors of fossils sat with a feeling of peace, his hand on her behind, chomping on the sandwiches, not talking. Full of good thoughts they were—collectors of memories.

Back in town Marie decided La Boite a Sardines looked good for celebration. It was half full of fast-talking and deep-smoking Corsicans, no tourist in sight. The hors d'oeuvres were exotic, just as they hoped: a umami-tasting sea cucumber, holothuria; a little pile of metallic-tinged roe of sea urchin; a fistful of deep-fried two inch fish to be eaten whole (they made the tongue feel hairy, a little); and some cockle clams. It was a pleasurable adventure.

"What now, after we ate the whole tidal pool?" Marie wondered, while Rob studied the menu: the main course would be raw tuna tartar, rosy, translucent, godly.

"Even a toothless jaw could chop this like butter," said Rob.

"It sprays juice at my palate. What can I say?"

The native red wine was black like anthracite, rough, but dissolved the mucus well.

It was difficult to understand the dessert menu—but they ordered from the whistling waiter one *Chock Africaine*—desert chocolate—for ten euro, to share. They whispered "paradise" in one voice. Marie paid the gratuity with abandon, the wine did it. And they were out under the stars, schlepping with uncertain gait to somewhere into the hills. Passing the garbage dump Rob hollered "Discovery!" There lay a thin twin mattress, looking clean in the darkness.

"We will sleep like in the Four Seasons tonight!" They carried the thing away. The path they followed led into a ravine, and up a hill. On one side of this very narrow canyon there was a wall of shale rock; the opposite side was a steep slope covered by thorny bushes. The ravine was not wider than 10 feet. After Rob cleared few stones away the geologists' mattress fit well. The bedroom looked fantastic, Marie exclaimed.

She threw her bra in the air, and it landed on a tree-heath bush (*Erica arborea*) famous for its root—*bruyere*—of which the bowls of quality briar pipes are made.

Then, out of the wind, covered only by silent stars, they fell asleep on their conjugal resting place, touching butt to butt with a feeling of safety and bliss.

❋

It was still twilight when the first bird calls announced the day, and then human voices woke Rob and Marie. The intruders found the geologists lying on their backs, arms along their bodies, as children would draw a human figure.

An Escadron of Commandos of the Foreign Legion descended upon them, backpacks heavy, weapons at ready, faces drawn by fatigue after the all-night forced march. They were far from Camp Raffalli. Their faces caked by dust widened into broad smiles while stepping over the corner of the mattress, delighted by their view. And each, one by one, pronounced few words of advice as to the positions in sexual intercourse, some of them contributing only one or two words of obscenity, but judging by their expression of delight the words were meant to entertain, with good intentions.

Learned polyglots and philologists would delight at the litany of utterances in lingos from roots Germanic, Ugro-Finnish, and Romanic; there was Wolof from Senegal and the Bantu tongue of the Ibibio of Cameroon, and there were Slavic obscenities. The mattress dwellers understood only one, it was the speech of a Slovak—their "language" being just a primitive patois of Czech. The whole event lasted about five minutes.

When the last of the warriors passed, Rob and Marie emerged from the induced stupor. From the near opening to their ravine they heard a brisk command and the Foreign Legionnaires started their march hymn, which gradually faded into the morning silence: "…we are rough and tough, no ordinary guys, our ancestors died for the Legion's glory, we will soon perish, it is the tradition…"

Dr. Marie Podbabska retrieved her brassiere from the tree-heath and with her man, Dr. Robert Cerny, they sat up. Both looked for words with slightly open mouths.

"I fell in love," Marie sighed.

"I am in love, too, my girl."

"Oh yeah … but Cerny, I fell in love with Corsica!"
They hugged tight, to be sure.

Killing Warden Polda

The villagers could have not appreciated the style but still, they were amazed to see Stanislav Jungwirth, the track star, running on the road just a few feet from them; they were amazed to see a grown man running since they knew that only thieves run. The champion runner's body was in perfect racing position, not leaning backward as when Zatopek used to fake fatigue, not bending forward as when Mimoun O'Kasha faded in an agony. The runner hit the ground not by heels but by balls of his feet, as African runners, or children do. His arms were at the right angle, he did not breathe perceivably, just flashed a smile at the open mouths of the rustics. He stopped at the first stall of the market.

Shooting out a puff of smoke from the exhaust pipe of the Jawa terrain motorcycle, the policeman who followed Jungwirth stopped the engine, dismounted, raised one hand demonstratively, and stopped the stopwatch with a jerk of his hand as if smashing a fly. He looked at the watch and announced in booming voice of victory: "Fourteen minutes and twenty seconds."

Chief Detective Inspector Dvorak, from the Homicide Division in the big city, leaned on the police car, threw the half-smoked cigarette on the ground, and spit on the butt: "Wasted time and wasted money, all a goddam waste!" It became clear (to those not in the know) that the killer couldn't have run from the place of the murder to the market faster than the champion's fourteen minutes; there was no way he could have run it in twelve minutes.

※

The problems for the poachers became serious at the exact moment when Frybort got shot. It was a flesh wound at the left shoulder, but only ten inches from the heart. After the shooting Frybort, who knew every bush and nook of the forest, easily ran away, waded through part of the river, crossed the quicksand of the bog through the narrow path, dashed through the bushes along Berthold's pond, and came home by the back door of the barn. His Tereza took care of him right away; she put aloe on the entrance and exit wound, and bandaged it with a clean stocking. The bullet went just through the skin—the muscle was not damaged. It looked good. She gave him a shot of moonshine, *slivovitz*, and did not ask questions. He did not tell her that Game Warden Polda did it. She knew. He told her only that if anybody asked she should tell them that he spent all night at home with her, that they were playing cards. Then Frybort got drunk to ease the pain.

They were not slaves and no longer even serfs, but everybody in the village had been poor because the soil was poor. In recent times of proteins and vitamins they were left behind on potatoes. They survived because the circumstances of life taught them to face difficulties with pragmatic common sense and apply generations of experience. Unsurprisingly, their priority was survival of the family. That was the principal all held forward and of which nobody talked. To survive in good health on a diet of only potatoes was impossible, so from time to time the man of the family had to set up a trap and snare for a rabbit, hare, pheasant or partridge. And once a year the man would unwrap his hidden rifle and stalk a deer through the night. He would then fire only one round, without a miss, like an Eskimo. Cartridges were expensive. Poaching in the State Forest was a crime to be severely punished, so only a few men of the village dared this deed—only those who knew the forest as well or better than deer.

Game Wardens knew of this tradition and respected the men's need. The men respected the duties of the Warden. It was normal. It all changed when Polda, the new Game Warden, shot Frybort.

Polda had come from the city a few months earlier, moved into an abode at the edge of the village, by the carp pond, and lived there alone. At first he was welcomed in the tavern, but soon found himself sitting in the corner alone with his tankard of brew. One evening, when drunk, he announced in no uncertain language, that he would put an end to the disgusting poaching here, even if he would have to shoot the criminals, like dogs. One by one people mumbled into their pitchers that it was unwise talk. Many said that the warden lacked common sense and therefore would meet an unpleasant end. That was certain, they said, and waited.

But Bouda, Frybort, Horak from the Meadow, and his brother, Horak the Fisher, did not wait. Frybort had gotten shot and things could and would get only worse, in a hurry.

They met after dark in Bouda's barn. They sat on bails and talked about potatoes, at first. Bouda brought four cups and the moonshine, and they drank a little, because that was how it must be done before a decision could be made.

The peasants did not call themselves poachers; they did not call themselves anything. They knew each other and their circumstances. They looked old, four brown boulders, their hands holding cups like shovels, with old translucent calluses, nails like claws, badges of the labor from sunrise till sunset. They were men with tanned leather serious faces, now, but they could be seen with a happy grin when they would bring a carcass of wildlife to the table. The different body parts would be cooked in different ways; some with cranberries, others with mushrooms like chicken-of-the-woods or horns-of-plenty, all gifts of the generous forest. A stew would be made with beer. Kids would get the brain scrambled with eggs, would suck the marrow out of bones, a rare delicacy. It would be something to remember for the whole potato year.

But tonight the men knew what had to be decided. Bouda brought three green marbles and one yellow—the sulphur butterfly marble would kill Warden Polda. Bouda put the marbles in his cup, still wet with slivovitz, and looked at his friends. They all knew what to do. One by one they reached in and pulled out green marble, Frybort pulled out the yellow. Nobody moved even a brow, nobody said a word. Frybort's eyes remained calm, only his lips tightened and quivered for a short second. His infantile porcelain-blue eyes said nothing, his corrugated brow remained low.

Bouda smashed the cup on the floor where it shattered. All eyes were on the shards, and nobody looked up, nobody looked at Frybort. *Alea iacta est*—done deal. Bouda got up silently, put his hand on Frybort's shoulder. Then Horak from the Meadow talked briefly: "No gun must be used. No shooting." His eyes met Frybort's, who acknowledged understanding with a nod. "Too dangerous, too dangerous to make such noise, they would come searching for our guns."

❈

Polda rarely deviated from his daily routine. From the morning inspection he would return at about nine. He stopped in the Pub for a sausage and a pint, talked to nobody, went home. Frybort did not know the meaning of the verb "to study," but study he did, every step of his victim. It was the first market day, he decided, that was most suitable for his task, since everybody would be going to the joyous occasion to meet neighbors, and to buy a few trinkets or necessities.

Rosie, the train station attendant, related the event to the police in great detail, she stressed the accuracy of timing. She came out of her booth to accept the train from Jarosov. The local was again on time, arriving at 9:20 AM. Just before the train arrived Rosie saw everything, she said.

"I recognized warden Polda coming up the path along the forest to the station. Then I saw a man stepping out of the bushes, he approached Polda from behind and hit him over the head. Twice."

Rosie described the assailant as of medium height, wearing a black cap, with scarf wrapped over his face. With obvious pleasure at her ability to describe the details, she said that it was the first blow of the stick (it was a heavy ax handle found later next to the dead body) that got Polda to his knees, his hat blown away. The killer then struck a second blow; the warden fell flat down, motionless. After she dispatched the train, Rosie ran to the telephone to call police. When she came out again the killer had gone, disappeared into the forest. The Warden remained still.

"The time of the killing, Chief, was exactly at 9:18 AM. That is a fact," Rosie said.

❄

It took less than a minute, but it was hard. The second blow was powerful, it split the Warden's head and Polda slumped forward, remained motionless. Frybort looked around, saw the train leaving the station and knew he could have been seen. Old hunters do not panic. He checked his clothes—there was no blood or brain on him. He took off his gloves, put them in his pocket and started running. He ran the "Indian way," alternating a few paces of jogging with few paces of walking. His plan was thought out well, as well as the hunt for a wild boar. He emerged from the eastern edge of the pine growth and crossed the unfenced yard of the Pragers' summer home; he knew they were still in Prague. Then he crossed Blaha's pear orchard and ran over the bridge. The bridge was the only place that he could have been seen on this shortcut he choose, but he rightly expected that everybody would already be at the market. He threw his cap into the river.

He emerged at the market greeted by neighbors, approached his almost-friend, Constable Pivonka, who was watching the very high bottom of widow Maruska, and asked him the time. The Constable woke up from his dream: "Exactly half past nine, Frybort, but we expect the Mayor from the city at ten, so no hurry." He saluted his friend smartly, in a joking way. Frybort thanked him and then he bought a sugar-coated gingerbread heart for his little girl.

That same day the team of the Homicide Division from the District Capitol arrived in two cars, speeding through the village, driving the street poultry into a panic. The investigation started immediately. Photographs were made of the crime scene and the corpse, the ax handle was dusted for fingerprints, tracks in the dusty path were looked for—but the search did not result in any useful information. Rosie from the train station was repeatedly interviewed; she remembered all the details, and felt very important since she saw the deed and knew exactly the time. A few times she altered the description of the assailant, but neither of her variations was helpful: the man she described was nondescript, ageless, of medium height, sort of … he was not different, she said.

Chief Detective Inspector Dvorak was not a happy camper, as the saying goes. He called his deputies to his office and insulted them as usual, since the interviews of the usual suspects in the village had not yielded much, either, with one exception. The Horak brothers were seen by many, as they were repairing a tractor all morning, Blaha was in the city in the tax office from 9 o'clock. But Frybort was gone—picking mushrooms, he insisted. That was a great lead! So Frybort was called in and interrogated by the old-fashioned method of bad cop-good cop that Chief Dvorak had seen on TV.

"So, Frybort, how were the mushrooms? Should have been good, it was raining few nights ago. Before the gruesome murder."

"No good, sir, it was not too good, death trumpets and destroying angels everywhere, just got a few ceps and chanterelles. Nobody knows when the mushrooms grow, sir."

"Is that right?"

"Yes, I swear, Chief. But, come to think of it, sir, I found a couple of the pricks—stinkhorns (*phallus impudicus*, Linn.). By the creek."

"So, you dick, you think this is some kind of fun, a kinda comedy!" The color of the Chief's nose deepened to a Merlot hue. "Well, we know what to do with our mycologist-murderer. Ha?"

"Yes sir, Chief." The suspect nodded in agreement.

"Well, you imbecile, so when you hit Polda were you sure you left him for dead, bleeding to death, you creep? Rosie from the station saw you real well, you sonuvabitch."

"Sir, Inspector, I stated for the record several times, to the deputies, I had nothing to do with the unfortunate death of poor Game Warden Polda." Frybort shook his head, his eyes lost focus and his jaw dropped about five centimeters to produce an expression of boredom. "I spent all the time, I mean after mushrooming, I was all the time at the market. Actually not all the time, sir, I left the market at about quarter to ten, went to pick up a container at the Milk Plant ..."

"Oh, so you have a fancy watch now! Is it some kind of Rolex, all gold and sapphires?"

"No sir, where would a poor peasant get money for a watch? I asked the time of Constable Pivonka at the market. He has a nice wrist watch, some Roll Eggs, surely, sir."

"And so tell me, what did the nice wrist watch of Pivonka tell you then?"

"It told me then that it was half past nine. On the dot, sir."

❊

When Dvorak threw Frybort out, he phoned Constable Pivonka, who picked up the phone in attention and saluting. "Yes, sir Chief, yes sir, I was in the market that morning. You know, kids sometimes might steal from the stalls… Oh, yes I saw Frybort, sir, I remember well, because we talked, briefly, I am so sorry sir …Well, he asked me the time, yes I remember that, sir, I had my watch on me…"

"And what did the watch tell your pinhead-size brain, when the poacher asked you, if I may ask, Pivonka?" the Inspector roared.

"Sir, it told my brain, the watch, that it was exactly half past nine—half an hour before the ten hour, on the button, of that I am sure." Pivonka stood at attention still, when Dvorak slammed the phone down. "I am glad to be of help, sir," Constable Pivonka whispered into the now mute instrument, and invisible to the Chief Detective Inspector, he raised up his brows and the corners of his mouth.

"Svoboda!" Chief Detective Dvorak roared into the corridor. The deputy appeared jogging and buttoning up his tunic. "Yes, sir, Chief?" He mimed a rugged attention.

"Svoboda, listen to me. Don't you have some of your people married to Jungwirth. The great runner?"

"Oh ya, sir, my cousin from my dad's side, she is married to Jungwirth. She is a nice girl, sir."

In a sudden metamorphosis from a vile-tempered sonovabitch to a gentle, accommodating friend, Dvorak offered a chair to the pleasant nonentity of his deputy and explained to him his stratagem. They would bring the runner from Prague to the village and let him run the distance from the site of the murder to the market, to see, by a stopwatch, if the distance could be run in ten minutes. And if it could be run, then Frybort could have run it, too, and would be thrown into the slammer for all the rest of his bloody life.

"I need the telephone number for that Jungwirth. We'll bring him from Prague by car, round trip, pay him 500 crowns ... no 750 crowns. Do you understand, Svoboda? Got it in your brain?"

And so it happened. The celebrated runner arrived. He understood the task. He changed into his fanciest racing outfit, bought in Finland, oiled his hair well, too. He waved to the crowds in a nonchalant way, even threw a smile or two at the open mouths of the rustics. He ran the distance in a medium tempo of training for a mile, and stopped at the first market stall. Shooting a puff of smoke from the exhaust from his Jawa terrain motorcycle, deputy Svoboda stopped the vehicle. He had followed Jungwirth all the way from the site of the murder, measuring his time. He dismounted, raised his hand with stopwatch high and demonstratively stopped the watch, jerking his hand at the wrist as if hitting a fly.

"Fourteen minutes and twenty seconds," he announced in a booming voice of victory. And that was the end of the investigation. Frybort couldn't have run faster ... if he had run on the road as Jungwirth did! The villagers just smiled their knowing smiles, snickered, and looked sideways. Silence fell on the village again, silence angelic, rural, secure. The peasants were of the village, so they knew shortcuts and pathways, used in their illicit affairs, secret rendezvous, or just to shave off time in transit. The only question they could not answer for themselves was about the consciousness of Frybort. How would one feel killing not a deer but a man?

After few weeks Frybort slept well, again. That strange sound of splitting the skull that used to wake him up in the middle of the night, sometimes in sweat, that nightmare subsided. The falling to the ground of a dying man he knew well, as he had spent two years fighting in the Sumava Forest with the partisans. It was a very good time then, since every other day there was a hunt of immense excitement, because a hunter could become hunted, too. And at the end of the hunt a man, an enemy, would fall to the ground. Never again in later life would these hunting men experience such a time of adventure with purpose, and with true pals at their side, as not only partisans but many survivors of Vietnamese jungles know (but would not confess).

Just that strange echo! The sound of a cracked human skull, its contents spilling out; Frybort could not get used to it for a long time.

But not for eternity, since that is the nature of a man with friends who put arms around his shoulder. And that is how time, the mighty fourth dimension, works.

Importance of the Craze

The bridges make a string on which the beads of coral islands are thrown into the Atlantic from the tip of South Florida. The Florida Keys are subtropical jewels, with palms of many kinds swaying and rustling in the breeze, the roads lined by exotic gumbo-limbo trees, Jamaican fish-fuddle trees, torchwoods, buttonwoods, the famous lignum vitae and other Caribbean botanicals. But it is the sea, changing from chartreuse green to Curacao blue, which makes the Keys The Destination.

Winds come from the north in winter and from the south and east in summer and fall, during the hurricane season. Storms come often and unannounced from unpredictable directions, so not one of the thousand local boaters and fishermen can be found without the weather radio, clipped on the belt, sitting on the bed stand, by the kitchen sink and always bolted to the boat's dashboard.

Jerry Pfeffer tuned up the Key West weather station WX95. The forecast made his forehead wrinkle. The digitalized voice insisted on "… small craft advisory! … east to southeast winds at 25 knots gusting to 35 knots, isolated thunderstorms, temperature of coastal waters at the Gulf of Mexico seventy degrees, seas four to five feet." The small craft advisory and high waves worried Jerry, because plans to go fishing were already made. It was the last day of his friend Vance's vacation here, the very last chance to go out for the big one. Putting out his twelve-foot aluminum open skiff might be dicey, he thought, but Grassy Key should screen the wind from the Atlantic side for some distance, so it might not be so bad a couple of miles from the shore. He'd promised to take Vance out, whatever it took.

Jerry had met Vance Bridges almost forty years ago at the University, where Vance had finished his PhD in chemistry. They shared many interests, including fishing, and they understood the importance of loyalty in friendship. They did not share the same political opinions, but understood that not all are created equal, and understood the immutable endowment of genetic contributions to behavior and IQ and therefore opinions. And in Vance's case—the predisposition to bipolar disorder or manic-depressive psychosis, which ran in his family for three generations. In this regard Vance was very lucky that he suffered only mild, mitigated symptoms. His depression was moderate, mostly just a sad melancholy, and the stage of mania passed often without leaving ruin or destruction to his social intercourse. He was a pleasant fellow to look at, smiled often, and his eyes were alive, one might say sincere. Because he was not a tall fellow, his protruding belly (toxic intestinal fat) bulging over his wide Bermudas was more than noticeable.

During his Florida vacations at Jerry and Alexandra's house on the open water of Florida Bay in the Gulf of Mexico, he muddled through the hyperactivity stage, not a real clinical mania. It was not totally unpleasant; it was just that some days, by evening, his hosts felt weary of Vance's indefatigable jeremiads. "I'll write to the President," he paced on the veranda. "I'll write to the Vice President about this," he bit his nails inelegantly. "We must contact at least sixty addresses about this health plan," he circled the dining table. "Yeah, I am going to start a new website. Twitter helps, you know, Facebook reaches," he stretched his arms to demonstrate. Far from immobile, his features exaggerated his words, words that often created more noise pollution than meaningful discourse.

But they were old friends, after all, and a fishing rod in Vance's hands calmed him like a dose of opium; fishing they would go, then.

"Thanks for the nice sandwiches, Alexandra," he smiled at the lunch Jerry's pretty wife had prepared them for the trip.

"Oh, the beer," she said and went to the refrigerator. She knew what to put in the cooler, had done it a hundred times. "Hurricane Reef—you'll like this beer, Vance. It is from a Florida microbrewery, in Melbourne, I think." She patted Vance's shoulder "Just be careful out there, you guys."

"Yeah, not a bad brew, but it must be real cold," Jerry added. "We should be going; I just rechecked the weather forecast."

"It should be nice—the sea looks calm, good." Vance went to the veranda.

"Well, that's just here in front of the house. The sea here is screened from the southern wind, which comes from the other side of the island. The Key West forecasters still insist on winds up to 35 knots, that is thirty-five nautical miles in one hour, Vance. By noon. We'll see. It's your last day here, your last chance for the big fish, ma boy. We must go." He did not have any beautiful thought for the day. The digital voice from the radio worried him. Small craft advisory, they said. In landlubber's parlance it meant trouble.

The sun was pretty high already, just peaking above the crown of the big gumbo-limbo tree. A big iguana came to take a drink in the front yard, a couple of rock doves were finishing the seeds from the bird feeder, and Alexandra made a roaring foam for her essential cappuccino in the kitchen. They loaded the tackle box, fishing rods, toolbox, and cooler into their aluminum twelve-foot open skiff with a seven-horsepower outboard motor.

Vance's mood was that of delightful expectation. "Ahoy!" he greeted, waving to nobody but a five-foot pregnant iguana on the dock.

❋

The going was smooth, at first. But after half an hour the sea became rougher, confused, and they could see the white caps on the waves ahead. They were two miles off shore, near their destination by the lighted marker FL G-4S, just past the shallows of Grassy Key Bank, when it became obvious to Jerry that the seas were too big and dangerous. Vance enjoyed surfing down the waves; he was not disturbed by the high pitched wails of the propeller in the air at the peak of a wave. "Whoa, what a ride!" The little boat still did not take water; it bounced, deceptively, like a cork.

"This is no good, Vance, we have to get out of here, and very fast! We do not belong here." Jerry decreased the speed, calculated the proper velocity—and more importantly direction of the boat between the waves. They could not turn back going windward, against the oncoming seas—they would be flipped over by a first wave. Wind abeam, that is sideways to the direction of waves, would capsize the vessel in a second—so the only possible way was to close reach, i.e. to go at an angle, and pray, regardless of their militant atheism. He changed direction carefully.

And then it happened. In the trough of a rogue high wave the boat twisted, Vance slid to the starboard side on the cross-bench, and the boat capsized and filled with water. It happened in an instant. Vance disappeared under water and Jerry, catapulted in a back flip on the opposite, port side, also disappeared, submerged.

The vessel was equipped with flotation material under the benches, so it did not sink to the bottom but floated just a few inches under the surface. The crew emerged with wide wild eyes, holding on the gunwales opposite to each other. The next wave carried away the cooler, (with beer), tackle boxes, bait. There was nothing intelligent to say, for a couple of waves.

"That was incredibly fast."

"Yup, I did not see it coming. It was fast." Then there was silence, just the sound of sea.

Jerry was thinking. He was responsible. He was the old-timer here, experienced. What were the options? The first possible action that crossed his mind was to swim for it. He could swim for hours; it used to be his life, swimming competitively. But with a look at his friend's head, the rust-colored thinning hair pasted on his forehead, eyes bulging in confusion, he dismissed the thought.

"We don't panic," Vance said for no obvious reason. He looked at his friend questioning. "We are not going to panic, Jerry."

"Sure thing."

Jerry noticed a clump of Sargasso seaweed passing by. It went in a northward direction and moved speedily. It meant, that the tidal currents were carrying them farther away from the land. That was not a good sign. He had been fishing in these waters for a quarter of a century so he knew that in this weather and high seas nobody half-sane goes fishing; their chances of being picked up by a passing boat were small, and would diminish as time went by, and the evening approached. He could not see any other possible way out of the situation other than getting picked up.

"We are not panicking," Vance came again.

They waited. Time passed. The waves increased some, but they got their rhythm. Only the foam which flew off their crests would blind them at times; they shook their heads, without a smile.

When they had been in the water for two and half hours, Jerry checked his watch. He felt cold. He looked at his hands holding onto the gunwale of the vessel—they were white, the blood drained into the inside of his body to keep the vital organs functional. Then it hit him: damnation! The deadly, stealthy hypothermia was creeping up on him.

At times, life and destiny can be expressed using numbers, ciphers. In some instances it is natural, biological. The water temperature was 70 degrees Fahrenheit (21 Celsius). For Jerry it was easy to remember that 70 = 7, which means that in seventy degree water the atrial fibrillation of the heart occurs after seven hours. Loss of consciousness and then death by drowning follows. $70 = 7$. He knew the data, the numbers from research done at the University of Minnesota, Duluth Campus. The research center there was even allowed, after heated discussions on ethics, to use the data from the evil experiments on cold-water survival done in Nazi concentration camps. That data was valuably precise.

How many hours remained for the two castaways in their near-death state of being? Jerry's calculation was elementary: before the night they would be done for; they had a little over four hours of breathing time, to watch the sky above, a few streaming wisps of cirrus clouds driven by high winds, and share some memories. Nothing more could be done. That is—if the bull sharks did not get them sooner. But there was small chance of that. Bulls are not common in the Gulf, and lemon sharks, nurse, and reef sharks were of no concern. Vance might live longer, Jerry thought—he was fat. A flock of cormorants passed by, low, almost touching the white caps of waves, free, confident. They could dive ten feet, take off from the water anytime; they could soar to the sky; they belonged.

Vance said, "We do not panic, we don't." His face composed a smile; he spit some water out, and smiled the grin of an innocent, unknowing of the important numbers of life in cold water.

Jerry did not feel primordial fear, or horror—he was overcome by sadness. He remembered this strange sadness, for he'd been in near-death situations twice before in his life.

Always the sadness. The feeling which comes after hopes diminish. He did not smile back at his friend.

Then something happened which cognoscenti in hydrodynamics, in the laws of buoyancy, in the science of wave dynamics would not be able to explain.

Vance swung his leg over the submerged gunwale and with great effort rolled over into the boat, managed to sit on the cross bench facing the bow. The boat rocked in the trough of the wave, the bow raised above the surface a few inches, then submerged again. When the bow lifted Vance picked up a plastic one-gallon pail, emptied it and started to bail.

"Don't do that Vance. It is crazy—just look behind you!" Vance did not look behind him to see the submerged stern of the boat. He was bailing with great speed, possessed. Jaw muscles clenched like fists, eyes almost closed, mouth shaken by inconceivable quivering, lips moist, he bailed in high mania, not hearing or seeing. The boat was rocking to and fro and water was washing over a bit. And then it stayed horizontal, for a few seconds. And then it seemed as if the vessel was emerging, first an inch, then three inches, while Vance bailed, riddled with energy by his episode of madness, this golden boy, until fatigue slowed him down, till it became obvious that the boat floated, only three quarters filled with water now, was not taking more water in... Vance breathed hard, ragged with exhaustion. With an amiable slouched wise grin, he turned to his mate.

Jerry managed to get into the boat, bruising his ribs on the gunwale, still shaking his head, pondering what had happened, in disbelief. Forgetting that dying was very easy, that the mechanics of their salvation was impossible. In miracles Jerry did not believe, but there was one feasible explanation, and he had to chuckle imagining: Neptune, the old ruler of the seas, must have supported the boat with his trident into horizontal position for half a minute to allow for the bailing to succeed. That old good scarecrow god of the seven seas…

"Vance, you saved the day. You saved us, do you know that?" Jerry laughed nervously, the first smile in hours. But there was not much time for talking. Jerry had to finish the bailing. It was an easy job.

"We did not panic, did we?" Vance whispered. Again.

The Coast Guard would find them, in a day or two, for sure. Maybe even this night with their night vision goggles, photomultipliers, infrared thermographics … and experience. Unless they were swamped again, gods forbid, then nobody would find two small heads in the vast space of Florida Bay. But Vance and Jerry had good thoughts: now, they would live to tell the story, they just had to wait. When would Alexandra realize that her fishers might be in trouble? When would she become so worried that she would call for help? By nightfall?

Maybe an hour passed before a thirty-five-foot fishing craft, with fishing rods in holders like the gills of a porcupine, outriggers for trolling waving on the sides, roared through the waves about hundred yards to the east of them. Vance and Jerry waved madly, hollered—and were seen. The boat turned around, easily disregarding the direction of waves—the three 225-horse power Yamaha outboards on the transom in lower gear just hummed with subdued power. Two very beautiful people galloped on 675 white horses to the rescue. The father and son were returning from way up north, from Flamingo in the Everglades, sailing home to Grassy Key Marina. With the twelve-foot open aluminum watercraft in tow, the two old wet men in it, grinning in unadulterated delight.

❀

It was a good evening; it was as it should be. There was a slight wind on the veranda hanging over the smooth water of leaden hue, the cicadas were at it, night blooming tropical jasmine scented the breeze, and an occasional bat acrobat hit a moth in a loop. Beautiful Alexandra, still shaking her head, joined them with a glass of Australian red. She'd got her boys back alive and breathing regularly. Vance was quiet for a change. His mania, which, without the slightest doubt had saved their lives, subsided, worn out. Jerry refilled his friend's glass with a "Papa-double" he'd prepared.

"You were one thousand per cent, my friend. The most number one sailor-man! So here is to you. Here is to us ... well, there is none like you!"

The blank-featured face of the No. 1 sailor did not move. But his eyes narrowed. It was a smile. He pointed with his glass at the purple western horizon. And nodded at Jerry.

"Yes," Jerry agreed. "Red sky at night—sailors' delight, as they say."

The Woman Who Knew 1005 Males

With my friend Vojta I go to the old-fashioned café Slavia often. He likes the Riesling they serve there at perfect temperature; I like the view of the river Vltava and Prague Castle, and the large painting of the absinthe drinker with his melancholic face as green as the face of Vodnik, the water sprite of Czech fairytales.

That day Vojta arrived on time, as usual—I watched the clock. We have agreed that only imbeciles come late to meet their friends. (Vojta often quotes what he claims is an old Celtic proverb: "The idiot who lets you wait—with wrathful skunk deserveth date".) Right away I noticed he had not shaven for a couple of days. He knows that stubby hirsutism goes well with his sharp features, pale aquamarine eyes and disobedient black hair disheveled artificially. Handsome devil. We greeted one another mutely with smile, adding "Howareyou old loser."

"I need an alcoholic beverage, fast. Otherwise I cannot talk".

"I ordered Ruland gray, already, worry none. It is the same as Pinot Grigio."

"Good vino," he said. "You are a true letrado y catedratico, compadre!" (He had just returned from Barcelona.)

Then we looked at each other in silence, since silence between us substitutes for bullshit, it is good. My friend is a psychiatrist, so I like to hear from him any recent news about the prefrontal cortex, where all our conspiracies begin, and about the hippocampus, the traitor which ruins our memory. So after a few obligatory obscene utterances I learned the latest news: "That 'noise' on the EEG, electroencephalogram, which we always thought is just some technical shit in the machine, revealed itself to be the real recording of brain action. You know, like, the brain works all the time, without interruption, the electrons flying like mad, chemistry blasting the receptors—day and night... I need another glass. Why didn't we order the whole bottle?"

"Wow," I said and called the waiter, remembering not to click fingers. The sun peeked in all of a sudden, and it was great. The gray wine worked our circulation, and the brain waves, too. The sun rays made diamonds in our wine and I felt how cool it was to sit with a real friend in Slavia, with the view costing a million bucks, under the scrutiny of the absinthe drinker with the greenish face of Vodnik, who seemed to accept now his permanent situation with just a scintilla of satisfaction.

We drank and talked about the invasion of mohammedans, the racism of Koreans, the danger of goodness, the psychology under a niqab, keffiyeh and push-up bra. The latest results from the Alpine Skiing World Cup affirmed our passionate love for Lindsey Vonn.

"And what's new with you?" Vojta asked.

"Well, I can tell you that absolutely nothing is new with me, nothing even remotely interesting, nothing to accelerate the electrons of my soul, if you will."

"Interesting? Nothing interesting in your life? I'll fix it," Vojta exclaimed in a mocking voice. "I brought with me an idea today: do you want to meet an interesting woman?" He leaned forward and a smile as wide as chimpanzee's grin distorted his face.

"Knowing you, I suspect a trick, some wily gimmick for certain."

I waited for more information from him; he knew I waited for him to say more, so he let me hang there suspended, knowing I would not ask. We settled the bill, going Dutch, and left in silence. Before we parted outside he said he would make arrangements, and would call me about the details, soon. "It should be nice," he muttered with one eye closed in the primitive gesture of conspiracy. "My friend, you'll meet the woman who saw 1005 dicks. Before she was twenty-five years old. Goodbye."

I am a man of science—so I think of unproven hypotheses and proven theories in terms of numbers, and consider statistical methods to be indispensable tools of rational thought and phenomena. Shit, that is why I am an atheist and skeptic—but 1005! I developed a few hypotheses about the mysterious woman, finding some of them plausible but none satisfactory. I divided 1005 by 365, by the number of weeks in eight to ten years. I applied tests for significance in small numbers and large, and I allowed for statistical bias. But the less I could corroborate my musing the more I was looking forward for meeting the woman, the real thing.

A telephone call abolished my suspicion of a hoax. The dinner date had been arranged for the last day of May, in Old Vicary, a garden restaurant in the Hanspaulka quarter of Prague. I arrived there first, taking the chair not facing the falling sun, so my wrinkles and creases would not be enhanced. I dressed carefully for the occasion, so my linen jacket was wrinkled appropriately; with my black shirt I allowed a cravat of bounteously colorful pattern. I found the table under a large canopy, which used to conceal anti-aircraft cannons or howitzers and was spread above the garden, creating bizarre shadows like Rorschach inkblots, which moved erratically, adding to my nervousness. It was a warm, pleasant evening though.

Vojta entered first, stepping slightly sideways, in a crab-like fashion, which I diagnosed as an excessive self-consciousness. She followed at an easy pace, watching her steps, in "sensible shoes", black stockings, a bluish skirt with its inverted pleats hitting the middle of her calves, and a unisex sweater of non-descript color with a v-cut collar. They had twenty yards to make it to our table, which gave me enough time to rejoice, to exhilarate on my instant discovery: I recognized this outfit, this disguise!

From the "noise" of my brain's constant activity a clear, colored picture emerged: the memory of a *schoolteacher*! I knew this woman's trick. I'd seen this ingenious harlequinade before!

I visualized the Rue Saint-Denis, by the 1st Arrondissement in Paris, not far from the railroad station. It was near midnight, the gas-lamps softening the silhouettes and shadows of the ladies of the night lingering on both sides of the street, all smoking, in twos and threes, talking, short laughter or an obscenity here or there barely disturbing the peace. There were no clients to be seen—we were the only males. George Petitrosa, my Parisian friend, had kept his word, showing me the non-touristy, interesting places in his "city of lights"—and shadows.

Before we exited the street of sinful pleasure I became solicited, quite forcefully, by one of the sporting ladies. She wore a most unusual outfit for the occasion. Platform shoes, long pleated skirt, cream blouse with long sleeves rimmed at the collar by lace. Her raven black beehive hairdo was an obvious wig. She approached us unhesitatingly.

"Wanna fucky fucky?" she inquired in non-Shakespearian English, and took a drag from her Galoise.

I sort of apologized to her and we sped up. "What was that?" I asked, after we had escaped.

"Schoolteacher, couldn't you see?" George then pointed at another professional across the street, in pigtails with narrow ribbons, red-painted cheeks, white socks, sneakers, and blouse with a stand-up collar. "And there goes a village schoolgirl from the old times. You know, some johns get kick out of this mockery; we even get nuns here. Very popular."

This memory emerged in my brain as if filmed by a super-high-speed camera. It took less than ten seconds.

Bianca shook my hand lightly with a little smile. I noticed her 14-carat-gold hair made into a smooth cap with one strand disobediently askew, the straight bangs across her forehead in the style of the Cholo Indians framing her intelligent, quite beautiful face.

We exchanged greetings and Vojta introduced us.

"Bianca is not a Czech name, is it?" I inquired.

"It is not—but my parents named me Bianca because at birth my hair was white, you see?"

"Well, your hair is beautiful." I was happy to say something nice, since she, the mock "schoolteacher", was sympathetic to me even before she sat down. Vojta, who was observing me with keen attention, chuckled. All three of us engaged in witless, very small talk—even about the weather, for Christ's sake. But my curiosity about the amazing experiences of the "schoolteacher" Bianca forced me to ask several questions, interspersed with remarks about food, slow service, and beer.

"Have you lived in Prague all of your life? Do you sleep eight hours? Did you ever smoke? Follow politics? Is *svickova* your most favorite Czech food? Have you known Vojta for a long time?...."

After receiving affirmative answers in this questionnaire I knew nothing about her, still. We ate excellent wienerschnitzel and drank red beer at eight centigrade, with almost solid, off-white foam. The beer came to the table in heavy tankards, one after the other, without us ordering it. I noticed that Bianca had short unpainted nails, did not reek of perfume, had very rudimentary make-up and, strangely, one or two of her remarks on medical topics were quite professional. All this confused me. We guys had had three pints already, Bianca two. Time was running out.

"I know," I dared with a voice of an apologist, "I know that here in Bohemia, it is strictly forbidden to talk shop, to talk about one's work when with friends. But, somehow, I believe, miss Bianca, that you have an interesting profession, a fulfilling job which you might like?" I felt possible disaster coming now, asking this question. I held my breath and she saw my hesitation.

"You are right, I like my job, a lot." She nodded and I was relieved.

At that moment, Vojta, who watched me like an osprey aiming at a succulent sea trout, interceded: "...and she is respected in her field, big time!" I imagine she is, I thought—1005!

Then I heard the story, directly from her, a matter-of-fact account simplified, no doubt, with her minor smile on and off. I liked when she combed her sunny helmet with her fingers, when the beer she drank left a smudge of foam on her lovely upper lip, when she asked me if I was not bored, when she touched my hand lightly to stress a point. I felt intensely sorry when she had to leave us for another engagement. We got her a taxi and then returned to the table for a couple more half-liters of the brew.

❊

"I hope you understood what she meant by 'hypospadias'?" Vojta inquired. "The opening from which your piss comes out of should be at the end of your dick. Right? If it is lower, underneath, it is hypospadias, and this congenital defect could cause plenty of problems and must be fixed by surgery. That's what it is."

"Yeah, I understand that, but isn't she some woman!"

"Yes, she did a great job. Her first husband was a plastic surgeon and he operated on the wife of a communist general, so this omnipotent Bolshevik issued an order for one thousand recruits to line up in two batches, with their instrument out of the pants, in their right hand. That made it possible for Bianca and her assistant to check all of them for hypospadias."

"Holy mackerel, what a project for a girl!"

"Yap, and that resulted in the only valid statistics in the world on prevalence of this malformation. Made her quite famous. And those senile, macho academicians in the Academy of Sciences, where she worked, had to promote her, too. "

The beer did its job. Our tongues fluttered out of control, the upper eyelids sank some, and our general condition took a turn for the better.

"But I don't understand why she talked about one thousand—and you said she saw 1005?"

"Ha, ma dear gal," Vojta displayed his spastic grin and forced a chuckle. "I know very well about one out of those five I mentioned. It was very nice with her, my friend, no war! And those other four—I just made it up guessing. You know, she is quite conservative for a Czech maiden."

He put his arm on my shoulder to help himself up. They were closing the joint, turning the chairs upside down; the waiter was standing nearby, whistling and staring with an unpleasant face.

Great evening, I thought. I'd learned again from my buoyant friend things that would nourish my thoughts. But after we parted, like a creature from the Black Lagoon, a thought emerged from the "noise" activity of my brain, and like that monster it held me firmly in its fangs: How could I get hold of her telephone number? And soon.

Application

Of course I hated all Party events, as did everybody else, Party members included. This time the Communist Party City Hall Committee called us for the monthly compulsory education seminar, a one hour torture session where you sit gazing into the distance like an imbecile and pretend to listen with eager interest to Marxist and Leninist fantasies. Falling asleep would surely be punished by death by grenade launcher (here I exaggerate). As usual, those in the first rows would fake involvement, while those in the back fought to stay upright and conscious. I was sitting in the middle (as I try to be in the middle in everything, being a certified coward).

When the invited speaker arrived I was jolted into a state of high alert, as if meeting Golem in Mailsova street. She was beautiful. Black hair with bangs like a Cholo Indian, and eyes with a slight Mongolian slant that gave her an exotic appearance. Lips full, and cheekbones as I like them, high.

Party Chief Zeman introduced the speaker as an expert from ISML, the Institute for Studies of Marxism and Leninism. He talked to her bust, forgetting the audience. She did not smile but looked strict, standing with legs apart. Beautiful whore, I thought, but something about her, maybe the exotic mien, fascinated me, moved something inside my chest. When she opened her lips, the upper one was killing me.

"Comrades, our great teacher Vladimir Ilyich Ulyanov Lenin taught us that when 'difficult at the exercise field—easy at the battlefield.' So you will have to study hard...."

Pure bullshit and impure propaganda followed for an hour. I did not hear the meanings but recorded the intonation of her voice and the staccato of her words; I let my post pubertal fantasies take over, watching her face *en face* and her curves from profile. After the lecture I joined a couple of eager Bolsheviks and approached her with a question. I do not remember what I asked (it must have been some idiocy, considering the topic) because I tried to smell her. I concentrated on the odors and, maybe, detected a faint wisp of pheromones. From close up she did not look as strict as when ruling from the lectern. She even volunteered a small smile; I thought of it as a heavenly grin.

After this lecture I started an investigation. First, I got a list of the staff of that Marxist brainwashing institution ISML and found out her position was not tenured, but temporary. Then I contacted a high school friend, who had made it into some elevated position in the Party. He found out she came from a bourgeois family, left home early to distance herself from her capitalist origins, and started to climb the Party hierarchy. She concealed her intentions skillfully, but still she was known as very ambitious and smart and an expert in making connections with the important allies. "A bitch," my friend said.

But, though it may sound crazy, I was falling in some sort of love by the second lecture of hers. I was in love with her physiognomy and her physique, her smile included. Then I learned she might have a boyfriend, somebody from the high ranks in the Party. But I was determined to erase this from my clouded mind, as a simpleton will do, not considering the possibility of my destruction when getting involved. Boyfriend? Is he boy or friend, or both, or some geezer from Council of People's Commissars with power? I'll deal with this later.

After her second lecture I humiliated myself and asked about the imperialist crimes of King Leopold II in the Belgian Congo, hoping to evoke her sympathy. For my submissive bullshit I was rewarded by a smile so sunny it made her Marxism-Leninism sound like a mellow lullaby. I knew by then, that all would be decided, and my fate sealed, after her third and last lecture, after my last chance to talk to her face to face.

The presentation about the working class struggle and the victory of the lumpenproletariat would have given creeps to a novice, but I just spent the hour imagining the speaker in a different position. I had quite a nice time. After the lecture I approached her and this time my questions were apolitical. I commented on her excellent diction, her rhetorical erudition and her blue-gray blouse. That, I imagined, should have been a proper prelude to the telephone call I'd planned that evening. Her telephone number was my treasured possession.

Evening came and I downed three shots of straight Tuzemak "rum" and then dialed. She did not send me to hell or dark place; she talked in a civil way, and I could even detect a melody of some sympathy, so I cut the nonsense short and asked her for a date, and she hesitated at first, but then asked when and where. I had to calm down not to sound like a teenager given permission to deflower, and I realized the sweet feeling of a victory. I felt like some sort of Don Juan, Casanova being an amateur in comparison to me.

The fateful evening of The Date I put on a black shirt, my only jacket without leather patches on the elbows, and my black imitation of jeans, then shined my loafers, brushed my teeth twice, polished my removable upper partial dentures to a high gloss, and cleaned my nails. Ready to conquer!

She came almost on time, looking nice, a new hairdo with those black bangs so straight they seemed almost artificial. It made me a little apprehensive to see her move without self-consciousness, cool, as one would not expect on a first date with a stranger. We shook hands and started to walk, not touching. After a while she stopped and from her purse pulled out an envelope and handed it to me without a comment. Ha! I said and asked what kind of a surprise the envelope concealed. She said nothing.

When I opened the envelope there was an application for membership in the Communist Party of Czechoslovakia. On the top it had the emblem of the star in black and white, with sickle and hammer.

We stood a couple feet apart and I could detect an expression of anticipation on her somewhat weird but pretty face. We remained in absolute silence, looking at each other, saying nothing with words.

There are about four or five scientific definitions of intelligence. The one I prefer, in combination of another one, is the theory that high intelligence is the ability of a person to adjust to changes in the environment or situation in such a way that it would yield a profit to the person or to his/her tribe and aid their survival. So to exercise my considerable intelligence (do not scream, please) I put the cortex of my forebrain into high gear.

"Thank you," I said, "I'll sign the application after you go with me to my place and we get laid." I knew my statement was as crude and as outrageous as the offer of Party membership on the first date.

She stepped back a foot and slapped my face with the power of a tennis pro known for a vicious forehand. It hurt. I swayed a little but I remained composed, I stood my ground. We stood like salt pillars for a while.

"OK," she whispered then, and took my hand. "OK, we'll go." She pulled me behind.

Danny's Long Night

He was twenty-eight, Danny, and two years out of medical school, enjoying all that the life of a young, healthy man brings. He was three years older than his peers because he'd spent three years climbing mountains and traveling the world. Women, his sporting life, and his friends were most important to him. He liked only a few men, but all dogs and all mountains. Six feet tall with Nordic eyes, he was an atheist and a skier. If one could foretell the future of a young person by their appearance and intelligence it would look good for Danny, unless he made a mistake with fatal consequences, as on the night we describe.

He did not want to badmouth this mountain. It was enough to know that for meteorologists she was of Siberian infamy, and was a part of the coldest mountain range in the country, swept by high winds and grim cloudbanks, most of the time.

✳

It was near the lowest temperature since recordkeeping had begun a hundred and twenty years ago, the computer-generated voice on the weather radio announced. The wind-chill factor was not calculated, since it depended on local conditions, but everybody who ventured outside knew it was pretty deadly out there. The mercury contracted to -31F (-35C, -28Re, 242 Kelvin). Wind gusts from the northwest could freeze a daring nose in less than a minute. Old-timers, who remembered freezes of minus forty, said that if one peed outside nothing would hit the snow; you'd hear the hiss of a viper and a small Agent Orange-like cloud would rise, then disappear. The miracle of sublimation! They also said that if there was no wind and one didn't move, the skin would not freeze. Wind made all the difference.

All this was interesting, Danny thought, but his skis broke as if made from plywood, right by the binding, when he crossed between two moguls—and that was yesterday, before the cruel arctic arrived. Everything was becoming fragile and was breaking. Not just the skis, but Lida's promises too. Something had to be done about these things—the skis, and Lida. (Oh, Lida-baby!)

That year Danny had managed to get two free weeks of skiing by being hired as a medic to a group of high school students on their Christmas break. There were two groups from the same high school. Danny's group of twenty good skiers were stationed at Sky Hut, high on the mountain, next to the gondola and the downhill racing course. The other group stayed down in the valley in the big lodge, about six miles as the bird flies. Danny had decided to travel down to the lodge, knowing there were spare skis in the store there. But, frankly, it was not only spare skis he desired—he also desired Lida, his colleague from med school. She was the medic for the group in the valley.

She was beautiful and highly desirable. He dreamed about her at night and daydreamed at day; he visualized her physical development above the waist, which could be believed only when seen, even from a considerable distance. But it was her beautiful face, radiating a high IQ, which drove Danny to distraction. Her unbotoxed upper lip was succulent, her impossibly high cheekbones were sculptured in the Dakota way, covered by peachy skin. Something to remember, something to touch. Her hair was another unusual asset: it emitted molecules of white gold, not some cheap alloy, and it was woven into a three-foot-long braid, thick as a gymnast's forearm. When she walked the braid would sway from side to side like a bell sounding an invitation. So Danny answered the bell and got ready for the trip.

He put on polypropylene underwear with wick action and a moisture-wicking merino wool pullover. Over it he donned a light fleece vest and, finally, a windproof jacket of microchannel construction, filled with Canada goose down. It was open at the bottom, per the wisdom of Eskimos, who knew about the importance of sweat control in low temps. Danny understood all about layering. The all-important boots with Gore-Tex Partelana fleece lining and heated insoles were carefully dried and warmed up before being put on. Over the Alpaca woolen gloves he pulled Swiss Toko mits. Finally, a ridiculous hat with mock-wolf pelt lining and big earflaps completed the process of getting ready. He would travel on cross country skis, not on those racing beauties but on the wider, wooden, tracking Finish Normarks he had bought from an ancient immigrant Finlander for fifteen bucks.

He started before lunch, calculating that he would make it to the lodge before dark, stay overnight there, drink with beautiful Lida (and have an *affaire d'amour*, perhaps?) and return the next day on the gondola, with the new skis. The travel plan was simple. He would climb up to the ridge of the mountain and follow the summit ridge well marked by poles planted fifty yards apart. After about three miles he should see the markings turning sharply downhill—the path would take him all the way to the valley, all the way to his destination, and dream.

He climbed the steep slope, zigzagging on well-packed snow. There was not much wind, and visibility was good. It was less than an hour when he emerged at the tree line and saw the ridge above. There he started to feel the wind, increasing in velocity, as he climbed higher. When he reached the ridge he realized the danger. He followed the markings for a short while before stopping to arrange his shawl around his face so that only his eyes under the goggles were visible. The wind was full of flying drift and wild, and soon his shawl froze solid as if fossilized, and was slipping off his face. The visibility decreased to twenty yards between gusts. It was high time to leave the ridge track and descend down between the trees where he could escape the wind. Also it was the time to decide whether to continue or to give up and return.

Danny knew that almost all the great mountain climbers, except for a few, such as Bonali, Bodington, and Messner, were dead. He knew that many had perished because they choose to continue in bad circumstances and not to give up and return. But Danny's problem was encoded in his chromosomes—never give up, never surrender. Genetic predispositions are an integral part of the hominoid genome and are often impossible to change. Thus nature won over nurture, as sometimes happens, and the skier continued. To descend through the tangle of dwarf mungo pines and into the taller trees, a stand of spruce, he had to take off his skis. The wind had subsided in the forest and in the silent stillness Danny knew he had got a chance. He would follow parallel to the line of the ridge in the forest in a general eastward direction—till he happened upon the path going straight down to the valley. It was a simple stratagem, if he could survive the cold. His toes and fingers were still in good shape. He put the skis over his shoulder and started walking at a heartbreakingly slow pace, since the snow was up to his knees, and in some places even higher. The darkness descended but the moon was up, so he could see well. Every twenty minutes he stopped and sat on his skis, gasping for breath. After trudging for some time he checked his watch—it was midnight.

When in front of him the ground surprisingly rose up, quite steeply, he realized he was lost. He staggered a few paces up the steep slope, and then stopped. With nagging uncertainty he made another decision: he would change the plan to merely survive. He would not aim directly for the lodge, but aim for survival. From now on he would follow a descending line, going always down the slope, which should take him to the valley. He believed.

Surrender? Never, he hollered, and howled like a wolf. He could not pin down any particular thought; he merely found he was laughing. Decisions made him comfortable, as any decision always won over uncertainty.

He sat down for a while. Had he lived long enough? But what is enough? Does one count adventures, loves, achievements, or just years, which disappear into the abyss of fourth dimension, the abyss that is the same for all? Are all lives equally precious when counting only chronology, the passing time? After checking the time again (it was two o'clock) he started. Laboriously he was able to put one foot before the other in the deep snow. He felt very alone, unreachable, like a banished untouchable; he needed a friend. So he just made up one. He called him Professor Bubele, just B for short.

B became a sympathetic companion, ready to argue, discuss, even to listen to intimate confessions, just like a real, true friend. His task was to make Danny less lonely, to distract him from deleterious thoughts.

"Worry none, we're gonna make it, Danny boy. Remember your crazy Fuji-yama climb?"

"Surely." Danny smiled at the memory and told the story to the trees and his illusory friend. "It was in December, and the Fuji volcano, extinct as the samurai but beautifully photogenic in her majestic snowy cape, was forbidden to climb because it was too dangerous in winter. Many corpses would have to be recovered in the spring. It was strictly prohibited, and enforced by guards stationed on the mountain throughout the winter. It took me hours to reach the fifth "station," Go-gome, from down Kawaguchiko-shi town. There were twelve "stations" on the marked track to the summit. They were resting places, some with little huts. And at the fifth station, Go-gome, at the tree line, there was a little house for the guard, who stayed there to make sure nobody ventured beyond him. He sympathized with me, since he knew I could not make it all the way down to Kawaguchiko, at the same evening. And the idea that this stranger—*gaijin*—planned to summit never occurred to him. So he let me stay with him overnight in his overheated shelter. He pointed to the tatami mat in the corner, threw me a pillow, returned to his cot to watch sumo wrestling on the TV hanging above his bed. He was chain-smoking and motionless, till eleven o'clock, when he said good night, *oyasumi nasai*, and instantly started snoring. I set my wristwatch alarm (which does not chime but vibrates) to one thirty AM, since I calculated that the guard's second period of stage three sleep, after the first REM stage, would begin by then. I would sneak out, scurrying silently like a bat. Which I did, on time, and in pretty good visibility I started the climb on the well-marked track, excited at being alone and free on the whole Fuji-san, the love affair of Japan, which would now be solely mine. The feeling of exalted freedom on my solo climb was indescribable.

"The trouble started at about the eighth station, Hachi-gome. An ice sheet covered everything like a white crusty frosting on a cake. The track disappeared. I had to put on crampons and to really start paying attention. Then my ice ax slipped off my hand and vanished, clanking. Obviously this should have been the time to return. But, my dear B, because of my cognitive deficiency and pathological lack of fear—I continued crawling upwards. I clenched my jaws.

"To complicate my efforts, a thick fog descended, and the visibility decreased to just a few yards. I crawled on my belly, grateful for an occasional rock protruding through the ice cover, and propelled by a flood of adrenalin I continued. I knew with certainty that a slip would finish my ascent and my life. But the toes of my crampons held well in the ice, every move I made was in the slow motion of a chameleon, thought out, deliberate. I eventually found myself in a place where the slope suddenly leveled, and flattened, so I could stand up. I had reached the rim of the summit. I stood there awhile in the dense fog; I did not celebrate, just felt proud—and only for a short while. Quickly I became truly afraid, since I knew that many a climber perished on the descent, on the way down, rather than on the ascent. Only a fool is not afraid. Or he or she does not know enough. That is what true mountaineers say.

"The way down Fuji mountain was another story of good fortune smiling at me. What do you say, B, will we make it tonight?"

For a moment neither of them spoke, thinking, perhaps.

"Sure thing, Danny. All it will take is reason, presence of mind, and slow progress. You must carry some very nice mutation in the 'Lucky' gene, Danny. I'm glad I followed you."

"B, you sumbich, you never get tired, though," Danny said. And then it happened. Danny disappeared. After he brushed the snow off his face, straightened up, and oriented himself in the whiteness all around him, he realized he was standing up to his armpits in snow, his feet planted on a log, which spanned across a creek, which was bubbling hidden in a tunnel under the snow. A squadron of Guardian Angels must have made sure he didn't fall all the way into the water. Luckily, his skis were lying on the snow next to him, which saved him, making it possible to struggle out of the trap, out of the harrowing situation.

He sat on the skis, catching his breath and wishing for nothing more than cigarette. He realized, quite composed now, that if he had sprained his ankle, he might still be able to have some chance to crawl and make it; if he had broken his leg he would have perished.

Fear, which immobilizes, must be abolished—it would sap his progress. We should die at the right time, thus teaches Zarathustra. So in violation of the stillness, Danny hollered "Not now, we shall overcome!" Life began again. He was absolutely certain. Then he peed, (it was not minus 40 yet) drawing a yellow heart with enlarged left ventricle on the snow. He smiled (the first time on this trip), pleased with his urine art, and started down the slope again, talking to B, talking even loudly to himself, aware that the state of mind is sometimes even more important than the state of muscles. It was about four o'clock in the morning, his toes and fingers still in good shape, when he entered a clearing between the tall spruces. He rested, amazed by what the sky revealed to him. He had never seen a sky like this.

"Look B, my friend, the sky is not sprinkled by stars, it is powdered ... there is almost no space between them! Can you believe the beauty?" Lack of humidity, high elevation and no light pollution from a city allowed the night sky to amaze the traveler.

"Well Danny, life is an illusion—the stars make up only four percent of the mass of our Universe; the rest, ninety six percent, is dark matter and dark energy. You ought to know that."

"B,B,B, you are the most learned imaginary scholar I can imagine! True letrado, compadre."

"Right, my friend. In fact I am never wrong!" So, after near tragedy Danny and B, The Imaginary, allowed themselves a time of rest—and contemplation.

"Is there a god hidden somewhere up there, B? What do you think? Look at the immensity of the sky." Danny risked it.

"Oh, my friend, you know better about that three-letter word, 'god', and similar childish nonsense. We astrophysicists and cosmologists, we ask more interesting questions, like what was before the Big Bang, what is outside of our Universe, some ten billion light years away, and what the hell is a singularity, where no laws, even quantum mechanics, apply and time has no past and future? And so on, et cetera."

"So, B, what is out there? And how did it all, what we see and are, how did it all come to be? Preach a little, *por favor.*"

"You don't see them black holes, Danny, and nobody else does, that bunch of holes up there. Nothing can escape the black hole, once it crosses its event horizon around the edge of the hole, that's why. Not even light—as most middle school students know. But this event horizon is only two-dimensional—in our three dimensional universe. That is for sure."

"So what? Is that so important?"

"Well, you don't want to hear about Hawking radiation, 'leaking' of the 'hairy' hole, the Chandrasekar Limit, the Great Theory of Everything, and such. But we, brains, calculated, not just hypothesized, that there must be a Hyper Universe, or Bulk Universe, Parallel Universe, Bubbles, or Meta-Universe out there. And this other universe is not of three spatial dimensions as ours is, but is four-dimensional. And there an immense star exploded and its core collapsed into a singularity, creating a pretty enormous black hole—of which the event horizon was not two-dimensional, like our own universe's black holes, but of three dimensions. And listen now—after a period of "inflation" (we do not understand that well) that three-dimensional event horizon became our own universe. Got it? And before we'll get out of here the Big Crunch starts! Why do you snicker? You wanted to hear! I bet you are thinking about getting laid, again. Which would be good for your circulation, I guess. Shall we go, now?"

"Thanks, B. These were the sorts of things I have always thought about when looking at the night sky. Even when I was a little boy, I remember. How clever the astrophysicists are, and how incomprehensibly wonderful, but unimaginably weird, all this is—for a primitive like me. Pity, it all is a hypothesis, and not yet a theory."

"To me it is amazing and cool, too, Danny boy, it is as adventurous and beautiful as a great cowboy flick. Now say good-bye to black holes. Time is short and the universe is getting older than 13 billion, 820 million years."

"Right, let's go. The trees are getting taller—we must be nearing the valley." Danny sounded rejuvenated.

So back on their way they were. The snow was less deep; the going became a little easier. There was hope, definitely. Then Danny stopped.

"B, do you see what I see? Those two small bright lights over there, like eyes. A wolf, maybe, or even a puma?" He stopped, trying to focus his vision.

"No, ma boy, I do not see anything. You are just overtired. Just don't give up now. This has happened time and time again to single-handed sailors too fatigued and lonely. Nothing to worry about. Once a sailor on *Tinkerbelle* saw his friend climb on board in the middle of Atlantic. I think they had a pleasant discourse." B grinned and the "wolf" disappeared and they were again on their way, Danny's shoulders getting raw from carrying the skis, his legs wobbly, but no body parts frozen (undoubtedly due to modern, advanced technologies in cloth construction and materials, and exercising toes and fingers at short intervals). At the next stop he felt an urge to sleep. To sleep means to die. The urge stopped; he recovered.

❄

It was clear—this was a road, this was the way to the valley, that valley filled to the brim with hope. The voyagers stopped—with a broad grin on their faces. But there was wind on the road, so the scarf came over the face, again. This might be a problem, Danny thought, since wind makes all the difference for a traveler.

"Wind is a killer, B," Danny said. "We have not won yet." His watch showed five in the morning; he was seventeen hours on the way. Life is not easy, it ain't light, like helium, he thought and faked a look of determination.

"You know about the wind. Remember Aconcagua?" B said.

"Oh yes—I remember well. Do you want to hear?" And through the scarf the muted voice of Danny came out.

"It all started when our mountaineering club invited the famous Burghes for a lecture. At that time he was considered one of the greatest climbers, summiting all eight thousands without oxygen and Everest a few times. He made some of the first routes in Nepal and Karakoram, too. His was a great presentation with beautiful slides. After the speech, at question time, somebody asked what was his most amazing, most memorable experience, ever. Burghes answered without hesitation. He described how he reached the South Col on Everest with two sherpas. South Col is on the Nepalese side, just few hundred feet under the summit. It is in the infamous Death Zone, since the oxygen pressure is only 33% of sea level, and blood hemoglobin would be saturated only at 40%. It is the place you put your oxygen breathing apparatus on, and fast. Dead bodies lay around (some without boots, which were taken by sherpas). The wind is terrific most of the time. There, Burghes and the sherpas adjusted their gear before the last push to summit.

"'The sherpas pulled out a pack of Marlboros, lit cigarettes with a Zippo and had a smoke,' Burghes said and shook his head. 'That was the most unbelievable moment of all my climbs.' Applause. Ovations.

"It was there in that lecture room, and then, dear B, that I decided to light up a cigarette on summit of Aconcagua in the Argentinean Andes, the highest mountain in the Western hemisphere. (22,837ft, 7000 m, 40% oxygen pressure, 60% of climbers succeed.) There were five of us; two had climbed K2 in Karakoram. It took us two weeks, the hardest thing I ever did in my life, with 70-pound backpacks, through the rubble and scree of Valle de las Vacas, up to Glacier de los Polacos, leading to the summit, under which we put up two tents before the push for the summit the next day. Breathing was difficult and a couple of climbers had problems, though not developing true HAPE, yet (high altitude pulmonary edema) or god forbid, HACE (high altitude cerebral edema).

"I felt good, except for the major, major fatigue. I took a pack of French Gitanes without filter, hid behind a boulder, sat next to the body of a dead Chilean climber covered with stones, to whom I talked briefly, and had a smoke. I felt like a hero—as any mentally challenged weirdo would. After a few puffs I was hit by a gust of wind. It was so strong, it extinguished my cigarette. Then another gust, even stronger. I thought the spirits of the mountain were getting mad because of my sacrilege. I crawled into the tent on all fours, confused. The sky was perfectly clear, no cloud in sight.

"The wind increased to hurricane strength, and we all huddled in one tent, sitting with backs to the wind trying to hold the tent down. The hurricane beat us with dull blows, continuous, seemingly increasing in power. The leader then called through the roaring noise, that this was a 'survival situation.' Which seemed obvious. This is the famous Viento Blanco, he said. This is when about once a year the jet stream descends as low as the summit of Aconcagua. To kill.

"It lasted all night. The supports of the tent broke one by one, but we all survived. Everything outside disappeared; we lost the Gamow bag, the cooking gear, the other tent, some climbing gear—we jerry-rigged the one tent but the expedition was aborted.

"So, that's how those bloody mountain spirits dealt with me, just because I blew some Gitane smoke into their sacred, thin air. They tested the limits of our endurance, and we realized that there is no grandeur in suffering. I found it a precious experience mostly by having had the chance to observe the behavior of my colleagues, and mine, too. And that is the end of a windy story, for you."

"Yeah, comrade Danny, one always learns in stress—and it seems that the more dramatic the situation the higher the learning curve can reach," B said.

Danny ate some snow and plodded down the road, stumbling from time to time, drawing on the last reserves of his energy. But he was not at the end of his tether, yet. Then, in a moment he would remember for many years, he detected shimmering lights on his left, between the trees. "What a sight of beauty, what a sight of beauty," Danny whispered. It was like a Brothers Grimm fairy tale—warm amber lights glowing in the forest, like a lighthouse for the castaway lost at sea in a raft. Danny's brain ordered his body to dig into the last supplies of adrenalin. He cut through the trees, some *force majeure* driving him now, his fatigue evaporated by the magic chemistry of endorphins.

There it was—the Ski Lodge of Dreams, achieved with unfrozen body parts, and unbroken spirit, too. Before he entered he had the presence of mind to say goodbye to B; he air-shook hands with his best imaginary friend. He shed the outer layers of his clothing and entered in a large, brightly lighted dining room, heated to Caribbean temperatures. Stealthily he snuck in, secretly, and found a chair in the corner, where nobody would pay attention to the stranger. The early breakfast was displayed on a long smorgasbord table. Danny couldn't resist and got himself a couple of refills of tea with milk and honey, a plate of lox with mayo and dill, and few heavenly rolls. The feast made him certain he was alive and among the living.

He recognized some of the students, so he was sure he was in the right place. He did not need to wait too long. Lida walked in as a ray of bright light, her eyes on the smorgasbord; she got her breakfast, found a place, sat down and briefly studied the pile of foodstuff before she dug in like a famished truck-driver. The view of it excited Danny and he moved in.

"Danny, where did you come from?" Her amazement appeared to be sincere, her eyes opened wide.

"Can I join you, Lida?"

"Sure, sit down. No buses come this early in the morning from the Sky Hut station. Did you just drop from the sky?"

"Well, I just walked," Danny said.

"Whatever, but you look beat." Her strangely pale blue eyes narrowed in a smile, and because of that Danny forgot his speech, and smiled, too. She was too beautiful for morning. Danny's heart was racing. He recovered and they talked about things, ate, and Danny was very glad he had not died. When they stopped talking he continued to grin till his facial muscles cramped.

"I have to go, Danny," she said. "I have a morning class on gegenschulter turns in slalom."

"Lida, I'd like to see you when we get home. Very much."

"Yeah, me too, Danny." She stood up. Time was rushing at the speed of light.

"I'd like to see you—more than once, you know. More..."

The simple rhetoric exhausted Danny; he tried to stand up, he knew the next seconds were critical for his future.

"Me too, Danny," she whispered, "me too." And swinging her Great White Braid over her left shoulder, she bent down and put her hand on Danny's hand. She straightened up and walked away, leaving behind a man-boy with feelings of extraordinary happiness, one nanometer from absolute bliss.

On the way out Lida turned back and beamed her half-smile, which could melt titanium.

The Visit to La Casa Fitzcarraldo

The pupils in the eyes of Alicia Clara, ebony black and surrounded by irises of heartwood mahogany hue, gave one a look from the darkness. But the darkness was often abolished by her sunny smile, so well liked in the fish market. Alicia was a popular fishmonger in Bellavista-Nanay. To locals she sold fish, both fresh (some catfish were still alive) and fried. She sold her body, part time, to tourists in the nearby quasi-hotel La Casa Fitzcarraldo. She was judged beautiful for an Yagua Indian, with hair like straight shiny wires and a complexion of warm brownness; slim she was and graceful. She was always clean, with maybe a fish-scale or two on her blouse; she wore only blouses, never the clinging t-shirts, the ubiquitous uniform of women of the village. Only she knew why. Morning and evening she was pleasant to her customers—never would they suspect her thoughts to be murky like the Amazon, since she was not in the habit of displaying her feelings, or sharing her mood. Indijenas are like that.

She knew more about the Amazonian fish than many ichthyologists, which made her happy—and sought after. She could tell how many hours a creature had been out of the water, except the boto, which could stay alive laying in the bottom of the boat for a day. (But that one, the boto, she recommended only for soup—it was too ugly, too.) She had the best connections with local fishers who came from far upriver; some were *caboclos* of mixed blood, old-timers, who brought her the best catch, like peacock bass: *tucunaré*. She usually saved those for the local celebrity Don Huerequeque, who played the important role of a cook, under his real name, in the famous film *Fitzcarraldo* by Werner Herzog. He built a bodega in Nanay, where Alicia got a discount on Ucayalina, the beer she loved. She loved the beer because it was named after the Ucayali River, which joins Maranon to form the Amazon hundreds of miles upstream and from where her Yagua people come.

For common customers she still had quality fish to offer, like *jaraqui* and *curimata*, so good for a deep frying, but also for ceviche, the original Peruvian specialty. Flat pacu are perfect for sautéing, as even Julia Child appreciated, sole meunière being her favorite meal. Sometimes the large killer torpedo *surubi* was available—that one could feed a family, because the kids would be scared away from the table by its tyrannosaurus teeth. Festo vegan tambaqui was almost always a sure sale, wonderfully succulent prepared any way. The world's largest river fish, the pirarucu, she would never get—that was only for the hotels in nearby Iquitos. Of piranhas she would sell only the rare black; too many bones in the red-bellied ones.

Regarding the deals with her body, she had her rules, which, by the way, would not be acceptable in downtown Iquitos. She was no puta from Plaza des Armas; of this she was proud, to some degree, and it still did not deprive her of customers. It was all about her dream.

Alicia Clara had a sort of cousin in the concierge of La Casa Fitzcarraldo. He, too, was a *caboclo*, a half-breed from the Ucayali delta, up the big river. And Alicia trusted Segundo, since his task was to select the right customers for her from the guests of the hotel who asked about meeting a pretty lady for the night. He would take 20% of the flat fee for the service, so he tried. Segundo was able only to preselect the customer as being a disgusting slob or a non-disgusting slob—no weirdoes allowed, though. His criteria were crude, so Alicia had to use a comb with finer teeth. It must be remembered, again, that she was not some puta from Plaza des Armas.

So before her final decision she would sit with the man downstairs at the bar and get treated to a caipirinha. There she would observe with one eye Pepe, the barman mixing cachasa rum with crushed sugar and lime pulp; sometimes, he used white rum for caipirissima, or vodka for caipiroshka. With the other eye she studied whether her victim ordered politely, using words like "gracias," "gracie," "danke viehlmals" or "thank you." She observed if he drank fast, if his palms sweated, if he pushed his cheeks out with his tongue, looked sideways, or worse, if he would bargain for the price. There were other aspects of his physiognomy and physiology that she studied with her fish-eagle eyes, but after all, she would not reject a nervous overweight adventurer with a kind smile. Pay the fee of 150 pesetas or 100 Dollars—in advance, compadre! It's for Alicia's big dream! A Dream House.

"He is a nice gringo. And he seems to be loaded too, I checked his boots," Segundo assured Alicia one evening.

"I trust you, cousin. I had a rough day, and I need some peace."

"You don't come for peace here, you come for pesetas, some for you, some for me. Don't forget, *carissima*." Segundo offered her a cigarette, knowing she did not smoke. "He is waiting in the bar."

It was a nervous but pleasant encounter from the first moment. They were both hesitant with about the same intensity. He thought "beautiful," she thought "handsome." They introduced each other formally. His name was Hans and he was German. He was long, carried himself well, shook hands nicely, had no sweat. He must have been about middle thirties; his black hair attested to a non-Arian ancestor in his ascending pedigree, but his eyes were Teutonic forget-me-not blue, which fascinated Alicia, since in Nanay nothing was blue—even the noon sky was tinted milky, and jacarandas grew only in the precordillera. She looked at his eyes, not into his eyes, and forgot what she wanted to say. He had a small lower jaw, clean-shaven, not the usual few days' stubble to enhance the manliness of a "dangerous adventurer" who would from time to time present himself with new Abercrombie & Fitch jungle pants, a khaki shirt with an abundance of pockets, and maybe a scarf around the neck.

They sipped their first caipirinhas, which helped them to smile, while the second ones pleasantly affected their balance. Since Hans did not seem in any hurry, Alicia took care of the decision and led Hans upstairs to his room. There he sat on the easy-chair and Alicia sank on the bed.

"You are very nice, Alicia, do you understand my Spanish?" was the only simplistic sentence Hans managed, after a long uneasy silence. His Spanish was excellent, though.

"Come to the bed, Mr. Hans." She kicked off her shoes.

"Well, Alicia. I want to talk to you, you know, about what you do, your family, about Nanay… "

"You paid Segundo downstairs, Hans, now you wanna talk, just talk?" She shook her head and raised her eyebrows. "Did you pay just to talk? Well, you paid for my dream, you know."

Hans hunched his shoulders, then he explained his situation. In Peru's Amazonia he was traveling with a group of his compatriots. It had been two weeks now, and nobody would talk to him. He was mute for two weeks; he was alone with them around him. They knew he was gay. They laughed at him; they were against gays, and they might have even hated homosexuals.

"So I paid your Segundo to arrange for me to meet you. He said you are very nice, and I paid him so I could talk. To you. It's true. I wanted to be like a normal person, normal traveler."

"Did those *malditos y malignos* think you had eight legs and horns? Why did you stay with the stupidos?" She frowned in displeasure. "But anyway, tell me, why did you become a *mariposa*, gay, then? Much trouble?"

It was time for a break, so Hans pulled a flat silver hip flask out of his rucksack and offered it to his companion. "Pretty," she said, but refused a sip. She was puzzled by the situation; she was used to a different sequence of events and deeds in La Casa Fitzcarraldo, and she did not need to get more alcoholic confusion. As usual at this evening hour, it started to rain, first in susurrant whispers, then in loud tropical decibels, which reminded Hans that he was not in Munich's Englisch Garten but on the Amazon, an exotic beauty in front of him, cachasa in his bottle—he took a good swig. He knew if he could embed in his memory this moment, the sounds, the hallucinogenic scent of tropical rot, the humid heat, it would be the great diamond in the crown of his travel memories.

Alicia repeated the question: Why had he become *mariposa*? She had never met one. Hans explained that he was born like that, just like she was born Yagua, or somebody a negro, or somebody super smart—"you see," he said, "I have two brothers and they were not born like—you say—*mariposa*. They have families, love women and all that. *Mariposa*—I sort of like that name—butterfly, it is pretty."

"Well, we have other names, like *cocorro, marica,* and *danao*. Oh, I forgot , kids say *culi-flojo!*" She chuckled, tense moments over.

"Amazing," Hans threw his hand in the air in an amusement. "So many terms—it is just as many as Eskimos have names for snow!"

Alicia Clara did not understand "Eskimos" and "snow," so she asked for his flat silver flask and did the deed. Neither of them seemed to mind the silence which followed.

Alicia stood up and stepped back. She pulled her blouse off and stood half naked, arms hanging along her hips, with a questioning grin. In the subdued light of the room her breasts were of mutton-fat jade, suggesting cartilaginous firmness. Venus de Milo—except for the remarkable asymmetry. Her left one was noticeably smaller,

Hans observed with astonishment and clinical interest. But in a second, on the projection screen of his hippocampus, he saw Amazons, the mysterious fierce female warriors of Greek mythology, who cut off their left breast to make it easier to aim arrows from their bows at male adversaries.

Alicia took Hans' hand and put it on the larger of her mammae. She observed no activity in his jungle pants; his face displayed a reptilian gaze of indifference. She let his hand go; it fell off limply. Hans felt this moment was like the crossing of the "event horizon" of a black hole —*lamentablemente amigo*. Only trouble could follow. His mouth was a thin slash, his eyes moist, his tongue locked—till Alicia said few words in a language he did not understand, so he forced a chuckle.

"You are very beautiful, very nice, cara Alicia Clara. And I thank you."

They were two intelligent people and so by the power of their intellect they recovered and resolved the impending crisis with wide smiles. It was not very difficult; their mutual newfound sympathy made it even comical. A happy thought occurred to the now restored Hans: *Maine echte Amazona! Die Abenteuer des guten Soldaten Hans!* Adventure of the good soldier Hans.

"I have an idea," he said. "There is a small eatery called Rositas, just across from Fitzcarraldo. And Dona Rosita makes wonderful seviche, *muy rico*, I swear. Let me take you there. I'd like you to tell me about your dream house, everything…"

Without hesitation Alicia put on her blouse and they were on the way. Downstairs, at the concierge, her cousin

Segundo leaned over the counter and in a loud whisper, with an unpleasant amused grin, said something in his Yagua acid twang while pointing at Hans. On the street, Alicia asked Hans to wait a little and returned to talk to Segundo. "You shit-for-brains, you shithead, shitkicker, and scumbag—from now on you can forget about your twenty percent, you can shove it high up your black ass." This was the lingo of a fishmonger, which doesn't leave any doubt about the power and meaning of the judgment.

Perfectly calm, she joined Hans on the street, where the rain had just stopped and the breeze coming from Bellavista-Nanay was cool, scented by vapors of beer and fish, and the indescribable perfume emanating from the Big River. Soon they ordered Ucayalina brew and seviche for two from Dona Rosita. This common meal was made into a rare delicacy by the freshness of the tambuqui caught this morning, "cooked" in juice from home-grown limes, with slices of white onion, garnished with cilantro from the back garden—and it came with Rosita's specialty: fingers of yuca (cassava, manioc) boiled and then deep-fried in palm oil. As good food does for everyone everywhere, it induced a mellow feeling of mild happiness, the sensation heightened by the second and third Ucayalina.

Alicia Clara described her dream—a dream-house to be built on a lot near a small beach where the Rio Nauta flows into Amazon, still in the territory of Nanay. The pylons were already sunk in. The walls would be of softer but pretty yellow capirona, the windows would be facing east and the river, so the morning sun would make merry. She described stairs and an outdoor kitchen with a separate barbeque pit of clay and stones, and on, and on, in detail, her hands in the air, her eyes wide open, as if she was describing a lover, a newborn, a friend ... her dream. Hans listened with full attention.

"But the floor will be very special, Hans. It will be made of real stone-hard renaco, smooth, scented of sweet tobacco when dried, and it will extend to a beautiful, big veranda, over the water. And I will have a skiff tied in the water just underneath," Alicia beamed with pleasure. "And when you come next time, in a year—swear you will come, Hans!—you'll stay with us. I will have a parrot, a man, and a monkey by then. And you will stay with us four, and I'll get you a large hammock from Iquitos, not from that little shit Indios in the jungle. And all of us will swing in hammocks on veranda in the evening, with caipirissima. The renaco floor will be a beautiful purple after the rain and will glisten like dogs' balls, and you won't know if you should look up at the big orange ball sinking into the river, or down, at the most lovely floor in the world. In Alicia's own house." They drank to this fata morgana, to the proposal of happiness. Two friends and six Ucayalinas.

Then after the last gulp of brew Hans performed his infamous imitation of a howler monkey to the amused amazement of his new friend and Dona Rosita, who was just closing the shop. Then he pulled out from the back pocket of his corny jungle pants the silver hip flask a gave it to Alicia. "Presento from Germany, guerida." She held it like a precious object of antiquity, radiated microwaves of pleasure, and thanked him kindly.

Alicia touched his face in the gesture of sympathy for fools, then took his hand and put it on her breast, the smaller one. She started to laugh at her confusion; she laughed till sparkling tears ran down her mahogany cheeks—and Hans joined her, madly.

100%

Only on the fourth day did the snow stop coming down. The skiers complained it was too much of a good thing—forty inches of powder dumped on ungroomed slopes made it dangerous; avalanches were coming down, already. Andrew Lindquist-Johanson had just arrived on Homeless Man Ridge, but he did not worry, since high school seniors in general do not worry. He picked the spot because he'd heard the story of Homeless Man and wanted to see the place. He decided to meet Mark there right after lunch.

"This is the place I told you about, man. The story about that homeless guy," Andy said. Mark knew one of the versions, too. "Cool," he said.

Everybody had a little variation on the tale, and as it is with Cabernet Sauvignon, the flavors became more complex and interesting with time.

(Version one: the simple truth was that one day in spring, a few years ago, skiers alerted ski patrol to a man in baseball cap and jacket trotting up the mountain in deep snow, high on the mountain, quite far from the lift, off the tracks.

Patrollers found the tracks, followed them for a couple of hours, then lost them in the open, where blowing snow covered them. They called a rescue helicopter, which scanned the slope and located a man sitting on snow on the top of the side ridge. The creature moved, still obviously alive. The rescuers in the helicopter extracted the man, which was not easy, since he did not cooperate, being snow-blind. They flew him down to Big Sky and then by ambulance to Bozeman, to the hospital. As the story goes, everybody gathered in amazement around the survivor in sneakers without socks, tweed jacket torn on the back, towel around the neck, and a baseball cap.

After his few frostbite areas were attended to, and analgesics administered for the painfully damaged corneas, he was determined to be in good shape for surviving the impossible. Then all the nurses of Bozeman came to spoil him, combed his few hairs, applied creams to his face, brought tons of treats, and even sneaked a few cold Silver Bullets from Coors Brewing Company, just to hear his story. The old man used to own several companies—but did not know how many. He used to have a family but couldn't remember having children. He did not remember how he had lost everything in his life—all was a fog. Except a face, he told the nurses. The face of Naomi he met skiing on the side ridge of Lone Mountain. He always knew exactly where, because he could see her face through the mist which clung to everything else. He told the nurses that he went to the mountain because she would be there waiting. Of that he was sure. He was unhappy now and cried at night. He could not see her, he mourned, because he was snow blind—and then some men took him away from there.)

Andy did not wait long for his pal. Mark bombed down the slope and stopped just a couple of feet from him, stopping in a fraction of second, as if he was a rivet pounded into the ground with one blow. He sprayed Andy with snow, then took his goggles off. Andy brushed the snow from his face and faked a right uppercut at Mark's chin.

"Sickbird!" he said.

They looked at each other and laughed like madmen. Andy and Mark had started their (semblance of) friendship with lightning speed because they both communicated in simple sentences, sometimes with the word's meaning hidden even to scholars in linguistics, sometimes with just grunts and hand signs. They understood each other well, since they had no ambitions in life, save getting laid, plural. In school they both were in the lower fiftieth percent in social studies, because they had their own social studies. The boys loved dogs and all animals—which put them into the category of good people with whom one would not mind being cast away on a deserted island. When it came to their motor skills on snow-covered ground, they were exceptional; their sense of snow, coded by their autosomal chromosomes, allowed them to perform feats for which they should share the Nobel Prize for physics.

"So this is the place of the homeless guy?" Mark said.

"Yap, uh." Andy.

"Cool." Mark.

"Radical—let's do it," Andy pointed down—and then one after the other they dove over the snow lip and down the steep run with hotdoggers' exuberance. The turns performed neared smooth perfection, the skis obeying in perfect parallel that made them feel very good.

They were good skiers, and had mastered all the white-knuckle shoots, the black diamond runs like Kilifer and Calamity Jane, even Hangman and Lobo and Devil's Crotch, with those 35-degree shoots, which keep the yahoos away. They enjoyed the easy runs on the freshly groomed corduroy, too, where they could show off three sixties on the pillow lines, and those smooth-like-honey stem christies, of whose flawless elegance even Nureyev would approve, but could not improve. And when nobody was around to judge imperfections, it was time for crossovers, worm turns and outriggers. There was always the danger of being humiliated by being grabbed by "snow snakes" or devoured by "mogul rats"—in plain language: wipe-outs.

As the afternoon was getting older, and the repertoire of fancy skiing becoming exhausted, Andy's eyes were returning to the peak of Lone Mountain more often. It was reflecting the setting sun in colors unnatural: salmon pink, in some places with a blue tint, all sprinkled by blinding De Beers diamonds, Swarovski glitter. It had been a forbidden place for Andy because of the very deep snow, sometimes powder, other times heavy firn, and the threat of avalanche. Dangerous and therefore tempting.

The boys were down at the Poma lift station. Mark had to go home. Andy said: "Be cool. I'm gonna go up the Mountain… Just have to."

"They won't let you on the chairlift up there, man, you're too small. You're a nut case… Good luck, though!"

"Well, if I make it, we'll do Gas Chambers, tomorrow!" Andy hollered.

Andrew Lindquist-Johanson got on the Poma gondola, the first stage of his ascent to the Bowl. He tried to assure himself, that if it would be too difficult, he could always traverse, zig-zag it down. The sun was getting low. Andy was scared, and it was not the fear which induces a pleasurable feeling—but the more common one, the one which knots the stomach and lumps the throat. (He had a very secret hope: the chairlift to the top might be closed; he kept this secret even from himself.)

He rechecked the buckles on his boots and the binding on his new parabolic rockered Rossignols with steel edges so sharp a skier might shave with them. At the top station the Poma gondola jerked, squeaked and stopped. Andy stood outside just few steps from the chairlift going to the top. Blinking his eyes in the sunshine, he put on his orange goggles, kicked into his Solomon bindings and slid to the chairlift. There was nobody else going up. Andy had got on the double chair, when attendant said, "Hurry up, you're the last one." Then the attendant woke up from his daydream and called "Where are you going, boy?" when Andy was in the air already.

The top of Lone Mountain was very close and looked different than it did from the valley. A flag of flying snow decorated the rocky peak; it changed direction and size every moment. Both sides of the disc-like Bowl were marked by avalanche tracks, but the Bowl was smooth. Powder stuffed the acres in front of him, and on it there were no powder hounds to be seen. I'll be alone, all right, Andy whispered. Time was short.

He rechecked his equipment and started the descent by a long traverse of several hundred feet, then turned down the hill. It was not easy, and he almost lost balance on one wind lip. He did not lean back enough and the tension forced him to angle too much into the hill, his feet quite apart. As he was not relaxed (fear does that) he had to carve carefully. He corrected, and after another turn felt he might not die. He was getting more control of the deep powder; while knowing he was no powder king, he felt he was starting to understand the snow. He stopped to rest his legs, which were trembling with tension. He'd made it about half way down—a reason for optimism, a beautiful feeling of achievement. He looked around.

There were unexpected ski tracks underneath him; he followed their direction and was amazed. The horizontal tracks ended before reaching the edge of the Bowl. The tracks just did not continue—it was not logical. The skier who made the tracks could not have evaporated into the air, or flown away. Andy investigated the mystery and at the end of the track he found a man. The man was painted snow-white, without a cap, his hair matted by crystals, laying on his side, buried from the waist down, one ski sticking from the snow in an odd angle. He greeted Andy with the mantra "my friend, my friend, my friend." The man was confused but, it seemed, not in true shock, yet. His eyes were bulging out, but his nose and ears still not frozen white. He might have been about fifty.

"I'll get you outa here, worry none, you'll be OK." Andy packed snow into a platform, took off one ski and started digging with it. He dug like one possessed; he did not want to think about the sun setting. Beyond anything he did not want to think. He took off his parka, sweating. Soon one leg with a ski was free, then the other one, and then he asked the man to move his legs. The man did so, and there were no obvious bone fractures, nor ankles sprained. Andy thought that if he hadn't found the man, the ski patrol would have tomorrow, or day after, and be surprised by the corpse so intact, in such good shape. The man rotated out of the hole, and Andy helped him to stand, supported by ski poles.

"My friend … you are one hundred percent!" The survivor repeated this complete sentence a couple of times. Andy smiled. At that moment he knew he was the happiest human in the whole wide world. Hundred percent! (It stayed with him all his life.)

He led the way down, making a wide track packed for the man to follow, without falling even once. It took three traverses to the Poma station. The place was deserted already, but the red emergency telephone on one of the pillars worked and after some explaining to the patrol folks down in Big Sky, the lift was restarted and four experienced ski patrollers arrived with a stretcher and Hudson Bay Company woolen blankets in which to wrap the now shivering man. They gave him hot rehydration fluid and assurances. On the way down in the gondola the man appeared better; he was escaping the calm creeping state of deadly hypothermia. All of the patrolmen slapped Andy's back, silently.

At the down station the ambulance was already waiting for them; the transfer of the stretcher was perfectly professional. The saved man tried to lift himself up. His eyeballs were retracted now with the feeling of safety, and he gave Andy one hooded look and shook his head as if in wonder. He raised his voice saying: "You are a hundred percent, son. One hundred percent!" Then the stretcher disappeared into the technological marvels of an emergency ambulance.

Andy flew away on the wings of total, elated happiness, not knowing yet that the wings would change into appendages of Ikarus, when he approached his father.

❋

Andy, his father Johanson, and Marcela were renting two rooms on the ground floor of a hotel, facing the pool. Marcela was his father's third wife; she has been his mistress for only few months before they signed the prenuptial agreement. She was nice to Andy, but watched him all the time and everywhere. She did not talk much, just watched.

"Marcela here, she was worried. It is dark, already," Father raised his voice. "You can't think only about yourself, you know. Just look at the clock!" He pointed at the alarm clock.

"But dad, I saved a man's life.... I went..." Father interrupted, mumbling "Yeah, sure," took a pack of cigarettes, and went to smoke in the hallway.

Andy stood there for a while. Marcela watched. He took off his ski clothes and put on swimming trunks. Outside he imitated a vomiter's barfing, retching sounds, pronouncing unprintable words. The heated, lighted outdoor swimming pool was covered by vapors like those at the Yellowstone hot springs, a little scary, maybe, but inviting by the familiar odor of chlorine. Andy slid under the water, stayed at the bottom for twenty seconds motionless, then emerged with a happy face. He was not alone. A man of fifty-some years was standing near, the water up to his waist.

"Good evening, sir."

His face was not handsome—but interesting. Something magnetic in his expression, a half-hidden boyish lovability, strange eyes … maybe a shy grin? His hair was dyed, and he had good breasts above his belly. Right at the first glance Andy felt certain he knew the man. They exchanged few sentences; the man asked about those moving fireflies on the mountain and Andy explained that they were the lights of gigantic Snowcats, grooming the runs for tomorrow. He did not dare to ask where the man came from, but suspected he might be one of his father's business acquaintances. It was embarrassing not to know. And there was this southern drawl, soft, with molasses in it, which confused Andy, too. The boy and the man talked for a while, submerged themselves, and emerged periodically. He was a pleasant person, Andy thought, and after a while said: "Good night. Have good skiing tomorrow—maybe I'll see you on the hill."

He felt tired after the eventful day. He was climbing out of the pool when it hit him. He imagined the pool-man in a Texan's cowboy hat, string tie, that famous face—he must be J.R., the actor from the TV series *Dallas*. Yes, J.R. Ewing! Andy was absolutely sure. He turned around, approached the pool as J.R. was about to leave.

"Sir, excuse me, please, but are you J.R. from *Dallas*?" He grinned nervously. The man in the swimming pool was silent for a while—and then he confirmed his identity with the world-famous smirk, the scheming, seemingly shy, but villainous grin, which was hated but loved by multimillions of *Dallas* watchers, and had induced schadenfreude in multitudes just imagining J.R.'s demise.

"You betch your sweet bippy, mi amigo," the actor said and, amused, he grinned again.

Andy said "Wow!", thanked him, waved and ran.

"Marcelita, guess what! I just talked to J.R. from *Dallas*!"

"What?" She rolled up her Botoxed upper lip. "Larry Hagman? You did not!"

"I did. In the swimming pool."

"No, you didn't."

"Yeah, I did."

"Naa, you didn't."

"Yeah, I did."

"Naa, you did not. No way."

Father joined in, shaking his head from side to side, and mumbled "You're talking rot, cut it out," then slouched on the sofa, opened his *Wall Street Journal* and disappeared into it for the night. Andy looked at the ceiling, howled not unlike a wolf, put his down-filled parka over his still-wet torso, and sauntered barefoot out. Strangely, he walked slowly, as if victorious. J.R. was gone, but a half moon had arrived, bright, cold, and unsmiling, in a sky powdered by stars uncovered in the zillions by the high altitude. Andy found the Big Bear constellation and then Polaris—so south was to the right.

If learned psychologists and neurologists examined the boy's frontal cingulate and amygdala, they would not be able to detect any activity indicating anger, anxiety, or other negative emotions—they would find only a smiling brain.

Because the Hundred Percent Young Man had a plan, an Excellent Plan.

He had studied the map of North America, and measured distances to find the place which would be the farthest, most distant from his family, preferably south. Clearly it was Key West, in the Florida Keys. He knew that at the end of South Street, there was a brightly painted, concrete monument announcing The Southernmost Point of the Continental United States of America (and in smaller letters: 90 miles to Cuba). Next to this monument stretched the Southernmost Beach.

And on this beach, wiggling his toes in the warm, blowtorch blue Caribbean, with a can of Key West Sunset Ale in his hand, right next to that southernmost monumental phallus the size of a Cadillac, the new wonderful life of one hundred percent of Andrew Lindquist-Johanson would begin.

The End of the Party

The world is always beautiful at dusk and dawn, but even more so in the subtropics of the Florida Keys.

It was a calm evening, the sea silver-black, flat as a pond, the cicadas sounding like Stravinski. Mosquitoes and no-see-ums were elsewhere, so it was pleasant to party on the veranda of our winter refuge above the Gulf of Mexico. Alcoholic vapors covered the smell of seaweed rotting between the mangroves, and above the mangrove thicket a few bats performed their acro-batics. Accommodating my eyes to the darkness, I could spy a great white heron, who we call Charlie, waiting motionless in the shallows, only his head moving from side to side to visualize, in three dimensions, a blue crab for dinner.

Five of us were settled around the ipe wood table, all smiles and very small talk, at first. Mona shrieked "Give me another drink so I can talk!" and Rush, her second half, raised both hands and said nothing. Paul and Mary said they'd had a great time in Italy, but still felt the jet lag, and so I made them my rum daiquiri Viper Key to help them recover. The Viper Key consists of five parts, all derived from tropical plants, so it suits this tropical environment and dissolves all worries and mucus, loosens the tongue, primes the vocal cords and activates fast twitch facial muscles. Everyone talks at the same time, with a Viper Key in hand.

"So, how was Italy?" I asked, in hope of hearing specifics.

"Marvelous, great," Mary exclaimed, and talked about churches, streets, piazzas and pizzas in the way of tourists.

"Anything interesting? Like did you talk to people?" I interrupted.

"Yeah, tell him," Paul woke up. "About the two Italys."

Mary explained that if you buy a Lancia made in Milano, it will be as good as a Mercedes or better. If you buy one made near Napoli, Lancia-Sud, when you open the door the handle will stay in your hand.

"Yep, this fellow we met in a tratoria, he said that the North and South are two different countries. He was an architect, spoke good English. So Paul asked him how it came to be that Italians are so renowned for their design. The guy laughed, like we knew nothing, and he said this: that a kid in Italy walks to school through a beautiful renaissance garden, passes great baroque statues on the square, and enters a school built in art nouveau style, and on the walls of the school hang reproductions of great masters. The kid grows up and becomes a designer, and when he or she designs, the seeds of art history, subconsciously, sprout and influence his work. Yes, 'seeds in brain' he said. Isn't that cool? Do you know Paolo Pininfarina?"

"Who cares," Mona, Rush's wife, said. Then there was a silence. She looked mean, with narrow eyes and lower teeth showing. It felt as if an acid rain cloud had fallen on us; you can't breathe well under such a cloud, and it's poisonous, too. Rush showed no surprise; he looked at me and said nothing, as was usually the case when Mona was involved. She laughed briefly—not unlike the strange howl of the hyena, but quieter.

Rush is my oldest and best friend; we go back to high school. He's very smart, but not nerdy, and has always been quite popular with girls, mostly with those we used to call "sleazy sluts," who were the most important for our development. Now he works in research for crystalline and amorphous solar panels, doing well. We understand each other in almost everything. We dislike all ideologies, religions, nationalists and stupidos, and we like birding a lot. We love all animals and kill nothing except ticks, and when we fish it is catch and release. Strangely, in our simplified philosophies, we agree on the importance of being nice to people and of lying a lot so as to fit in and survive. While we both try to find the truth in our views, we try to make them as simple as we can manage, devoid of bullshit. He has been a very precious person to me, never too far from my thoughts and musings. Always.

I was so sorry when he married a gal he did not really know. However, I was perfectly aware that a negative, deleterious remark about a friend's wife could permanently doom a friendship in an instant, even if well intended and in sympathy.

After Mona's remark I got up and went to the kitchen for a plate of baked water chestnuts wrapped in bacon; I had heard the stove calling me. Rush followed me to get his pipe.

"Nice instrument of destruction, this. Is it an Italian pipe? I see the lucite stem," I asked.

106

"Yes."

"Savinelli? Such a nice briar," I said and took it from his hand.

"No, it is Caminetto, I think it is the second best Italian. See the bird's-eye pattern on one side and straight grain on the other side!" Rush changed his dour expression, and the famous smile shone out on his Slavic, round face. "And here, see? The open 'V' stamped on the stem—it is the mustache of the founder of the company, Grandpa Cuchiago. Ha!" Rush radiated, and I rejoiced to see him smile, for the first time that evening.

"Cool", I said. "Let's go back to join the party."

"I don't want to go." His smile disappeared.

"Well, Rush, don't be a baby, please."

Then he bent his head and said: "I'll kill her. I will."

My heart constricted in a slight pain, seeing my friend's hand trembling. "How Rush? With grenade launcher, or Uzi?" I tried to lighten him up. "Come on, don't talk rot."

"Not with a grenade. With a pistol, Beretta, Italian," Rush whispered and I pushed him out to the veranda since there was no other way to go, no fire escape, no theatre trapdoor. There, Mona was pouring herself another stiff whisky; she did not like the Viper Key—"Too much shit in it," she claimed.

I did not want to give up on conversation, so I asked Rush about his trip to London and Paris. "Weren't you in London this spring?" I pushed, and Rush nodded and with obvious effort started to talk.

"Yes, it was a business trip, just few days. And I took a short side trip to Paris, just to see the newly redone Picasso Museum in Marais. Yeah, it was interesting, but short." And we heard how marvelous the Marais was and the new museum, and how Picasso was all brains, brains, brains. And how in Montmartre and Trocadero float dark silhouettes, covered in hijabs, eyes on the ground ... in this city of lovers, of elegance. My friend lowered his voice.

"There, I wished I was in our cabin on Clam River, up North, on a sunny day, just birds and deer and wild turkeys, maybe the splash of a beaver, and mama bear with cubs coming to show off ... no hominoid around." Rush stopped, realizing he deviated.

"Well, Rush," Mary said without hesitation, "it just shows you how Europeans are tolerant. Tolerant to religions and cultures, you see?" Mary is an Assistant Professor at the University, so I couldn't help myself from asking her how things were in the Ivory Tower of Multicultural Sensitivity, and if it was crumbling down, yet? This sarcastic remark did not improve the mood on the veranda, on this quite beautiful evening.

"You know, Mary, I was just thinking..." and Rush could not finish since Mona announced: "Look at the thinker, the genius! Knows everything!"

"Be nice, Mona," I said. Not more; I couldn't. At that moment, on the projection screen of my hippocampus, I saw a Bacuba ju-ju sacrificial mask made of afara wood, with a cruel, toothless, wound for a mouth, black hollows for eyes, stained black by soot and human fat, rusty nails pounded into cheeks, each nail an evil wish... I had to get up. I walked to the railing, looked down at the sea. I felt the desire to be somewhere else, like Rush had felt a moment ago. I wanted be in the rainforest in Amazonia, in the midst of silent botanical riot, to sit on a stump by a fire by my Indian guide; he would boil coffee, I would roll cigarettes from the black tobacco for both of us, and we would hear parrots shrieking, a few monkeys in panic on a renaco tree above, a bottle of the cheapest rum, cachasa, laying by the fire, at the ready, and on the bottle a jewel beetle (*Buprestidae*) just landed, reflecting the flames in radiant emerald and gold. And there I would have no memory, no plans, and the coffee would be getting ready, hot and humid and wildly fragrant, and I would finish the cigarettes of local black tobacco for both of us, and lose all memory and make no plans, but feel surrounded by a great natural peace—not extraordinary happiness, but peace.

I woke up and looked at the sky—red, with a purple line by the calm sea. The Asmat cannibals in Papua New Guinea know that when there is a red sky in the evening, somewhere in the heart of darkness there is a headhunting raid taking place. I yearned for the cannibals to change their savage plan and I whispered in a muted cry: anthropophagi horribiles, avanti, here, come here, there is a good head for you, out of whose black cave without lips unfriendly sounds emanate!

I needed different sounds, so I went inside and put on a CD by Louis Armstrong, my greatest hero of old time tunes.

"...what a wonderful world... I see friends shaking hands saying how do you do ... what a wonderful world... Oh yeah." I thought Mary's eyes got misty when the famous raspy voice with the beautiful melody enveloped us all.

Paul started to talk. I call him a relict of Scandinavia because of his lanky tallness, big teeth, and straw hair. He is a reliable friend who almost never loses his sense of humor or his balance on the tight rope of politics.

Paul used to be the bovine inseminator in a big farm in California, where he met Mary, who took horseback riding lessons there. She finished medical school and married Paul when he promised to go back to school himself. She wanted to help "people", not patients, so she went to work in public health at the University, where Paul worked on his degree in genetics.

I asked Paul what was new in genetics; we now live in the era of genetics and molecular biology, they say.

"We are studying the evolution of the genome, and of the brain, at the moment, truly fascinating," he said. "And how the human races developed, and how the brain increased in homo sapiens."

I knew it would be combustible to go into the topic of race, and would create an even more of hyperbaric situation with drinks in hand. But I asked, nevertheless, how it comes to be that about eighty percent of blacks (black Africans and also African-Americans) are under the mean standard in education of the general population, in intelligence, as it is often called. Paul giggled nervously but answered.

"You know, all races are genetically identical when it comes to brain development, prenatally and up to about four years of age. But then the decline in blacks starts and—sorry about that—it continues to decline. It is well documented by studies of identical twins reared apart and interracial adoptions." Paul stopped talking. I thought he felt embarrassed, lecturing. He downed his drink and looked apologetically at his Mary, who did not look much pleased. He continued, bravely. "It is all due to lifestyle influences, family influences, and so on. Sorry to say, but it has been all documented well, even on the molecular level, the epigenetics is the branch of genetics explaining it all," Paul said. "I don't want to talk about this. Are we having a nice party, or what? I need another of those Viper Keys of yours! Fast!"

"Well, you scientist, you Einstein! I tell you the reason. You wrote the tests, you created the system. It's all is result of fucking racism! Youzer, youzer!" Mona exclaimed. Long silence followed.

I remembered how Rush had married this girl. He met her at a party at Carlton College, where she came as part of a package: a few six-packs of Summit Ale, a few ounces of ganja and no objection to topless dancing. They started dating, and we, all bums, envied him. She was quite pretty, with a delicious chest, long attractive hair and a lovely face, never distant from a smile. She liked and remembered jokes, liked animals, held hands with Rush and was a graceful dancer, too. But after the marriage, not many years later, she began an accelerated decline, losing first the smiles, then the jokes, then dancing and holding hands with her Rush. From a cute, lively tadpole she metamorphosed into a warts-covered buffo buffo. None of us knew the reason for such a rapid transformation. But I suspected Rush knew well; he must have known.

Not long ago Rush surprised me, relating how they had traveled to the West, through the canyons of Utah, Monument Valley, the pueblos of New Mexico, and how it was not a happy trip. And how, standing at the rim of Grand Canyon, he put his hand on her shoulder blade—but at the last second he did not push. I admit it shocked me, then.

I went to the kitchen to breathe again and I decided to make an attempt to salvage the party; I would tell how the last week I ruined the famous dish, pot au feu, just minutes before the guests arrived for dinner, how with one move I made it a mush, and so on, and I would clown a bit, too.

I returned to the veranda full of good intentions but found everybody standing, getting ready to leave. Rush looked at me, but his face did not talk, so I did not understand. Since I am a laureate holding the degree of Master of Bullshit and Administration—MBA—I thanked my friends for the very nice party. And bid them good-bye, drive carefully, happy combustion!

❄

I had plans to go birding with Rush to the Everglades. Last time we had started in Flamingo and spotted 32 species, including an anhinga, standing on the back of a ten-foot-long alligator, a male rufous-sided towhee, a male red whiskered bulbul and even the beautiful, purple gallinule (*Porphyrula martinica*). These were our pagan idols of beauty, which we worshiped with binoculars. But I had to postpone the bird watching expedition since I had to travel to Atlanta and Chicago.

It was about three weeks after the party when I returned, tired, home. I sat in peace, like in a warm cocoon, seeing no human faces and hearing no Babylon of business voices. I made myself a Nescafe and read Kurtzweil's book on the Singularity, nanobots' replication, and quantum computing. After an hour my head started to spin counterclockwise. I closed the book to rest my brain's connections and opened the idiot box, where a severe looking woman in a police uniform was talking about a double murder.

"...and the preliminary analysis suggests that the husband might have threatened his wife with a gun. She appears to have charged him with a meat cleaver, severing his carotid artery before he shot her through the heart. The murder weapon, a Beretta 380 semiautomatic pistol of Italian make, as well as the meat cleaver with a buffalo horn handle, were found next to the victims." She paused, shaking her head. "Strangely," she continued, "the woman held the hand of her victim; she may have reached for him in the very last seconds of her life."

The fatherly-looking policeman standing next to the policewoman added: "I can't recall such a bizarre double murder, not one, in all those twenty years with the Coconut Grove Police Department."

Coconut Grove, the domicile of Mona and Rush.

I wanted to run to the telephone but my legs would not carry me. I tried to breathe deeply. A pain in my heart kept me from moving, since I knew. I was certain.

In the following days the feeling of loss did not diminish. The pain was not as severe as losing a loving dog, but it tangled my innards into a Gordian knot, which would not be completely untangled for a long time. When I would go birding alone, the pain would come back; I could not see the painted bunting well, through the tears. It used to be Rush's favorite, the painted bunting. It would hurt, bad.

The Cell Phone Incident

Here he came. From the entrance to his table of destination it was about forty paces. In between, the tables were occupied mostly by tourists, many of whom lifted their eyes because his appearance was interesting. He walked with a deliberate gate, keeping his posture erect, chin down, as if his progress was of importance. It was not with arrogance—that would be a primitive attitude—it was with a display of gravity, his march.

His linen jacket was appropriately crumpled, with a black t-shirt and ironed jeans completing the uniform required by published writers in this country of Bohemia. A few of the onlooking locals might have whispered: a writer, man of letters, *spisovatel*. Famous, maybe!

He approached the small table for two where Ella, the American Fulbright Scholar, was waiting with a smile. She half lifted herself up from her seat; he reached out and kissed her hand. This archaic relic of Austrian monarchy mores was observed by nearby customers with questioning grimaces and sideways glances.

"I am so sorry to be late. The Writers Club wouldn't let me go. You know how it goes."

"Worry none, Doctor Cerny," Ella smiled back, "I just arrived a minute ago."

Convention was satisfied by few sentences about the weather and the Writers Club. Then Ella, anxious to learn as much about Cerny in the shortest time possible, did not hesitate with her questions. She needed some data for her thesis.

They were sitting in Cafe Slavia, primely situated right across the National Theatre on Narodni Boulevard, in the center of Prague. Ella had chosen this place because of the picturesque, beauteous views from the floor-to-ceiling windows: the river Vltava of Smetana only sixty feet away, Prague Castle of Masaryk and Havel high above the stream. Turning her eyes away from this scene, she could admire the famous painting of *The Absinthe Drinker* covering the whole wall. Besides the views she loved the atmosphere, filled with the scent of espresso and wine, and mixed with the scent of history, now rarely found in the thousands of cafes in this ancient city.

The history had been written by men and in the case of Cafe Slavia these were the notorious actors and opera singers, who after a performance would cross the street from the National Theatre to relax and with wine or cognac drown the strain from high Cs in an aria, or the convulsions from an act of high drama, or mitigate their stress with the secret embraces of a lover in the corridor leading to the toilets. So, there was dignity in the history of Cafe Slavia, which Ella appreciated.

Cerny asked Ella about the origin of her almost perfect Czech and learned, briefly, about her emigrant parents who remained so homesick they insisted on her education in the Czech language, and even sent her for a year to Prague in a student exchange program. Ella asked in turn about her companion's heritage, and learned that his grandmother came from Gdyne or Gdansk.

"I don't know where that is—but it must be a wonderful place," Ella responded. That stopped the discourse for a minute.

Cerny called for the waiter. "Dear Elly, would you prefer white, like the last time? Here they have nicely cooled *Rulandske sede*, which is Pinot Grigio. If you will. Not some *McWine*—one can detect the limestone *terroir of* Vestonice Hills. I call it the minerality of our Venus of Vestonice. Ha!" He altered the position of the ashtray, and leaned back. He seemed to be very satisfied. But not for long.

"Doctor Cerny, about that last novel of Ivan Prucha, what do you think? I know you read it." Cerny was taken aback; he expected to discuss his novel and not Prucha's. He answered carefully, making a few neutral points, saying nothing worth writing down. He covered his disappointment with an act of deep thought, and spoke about Prucha's failures in grammar, but his good understanding of present societal trends, which, however, lacked depth. "Not only the depths are dangerous, but shallows, too, if you know what I mean." He smiled, contented with his metaphor. This gal is different, he thought, dangerous even. At the Writers Club straight, direct questions were considered *faux pas*, low class. Ambiguity was valued, and the art of sarcastic bullshit with a smile or chuckle was cultivated. He was looking for a spark of admiration in Ella's eyes—but did not find it.

Ella had been working on her Master of Arts degree at the University of Minnesota. The topic of her thesis was "Postcommunist Czech Literature." She had been awarded the Fulbright Fellowship, which paid for a year's stay in Prague. She needed information.

"Dr. Cerny, I appreciate your candor, and erudition, too."

"Ho, ho, ho, nice to say it … but yes, we should talk from the heart, from right here." He pointed to his chest, then inspected the wine by swirling the glass. He talked to her loudly, as some do when speaking with anyone of alien nationality.

"You know, Ella, as I said, I admire your mastery of our language; it seems you understand its spirit, too. Fantastic!"

"Well, thank you. I am still learning, mostly from reading, and your writing has been of great help, too. So how about the novel by Prucha? You know how highly I value your opinions. And I need it for my thesis, you see?" She was trying to hide her disappointment, since in the last twenty minutes she had not heard anything of substance. All her companion's sentences were attempts to show the excellence of his critical thinking.

Ella had expected this failure, anyway. She had one close friend in Prague. Lada was highly regarded as a writer of non-fiction, and awarded literary prizes; her book on the collaboration between French writers and intellectuals during the Second World War was considered a definitive treatise. Ella admired her; they could talk extensively about serious matters in literature, but in the end they would become two girls, laughing and getting plastered. And Lada warned Ella about Creny's prevailing characteristic urge to impress.

"It has been his main goal in life to be admired. It might come to be his demise, too," Lada said.

Lada mentioned Cerny's suicidal tendencies—he would slip into depression, when his ego got bruised. "We all might have some complexes, hidden, in our pants, maybe," she laughed. "But his complexes get magnified like … like they are under a scanning electron microscope. They have taken him twice to the loony house, already. Pity," Lada said. "He is basically a good man. Never did he kowtow to the Bolsheviks. That took some major determination and character. And there were not many like that."

Ella had also talked to students in the Skvorecky Literary Academy, where Cerny taught. (Skvorecky was a Canadian writer, an immigrant from Czechoslovakia, who escaped communists, and a became professor of literature in Toronto. He remained very popular in his old country for the first of his forty novels, *The Cowards*, and for refusing to write in English.) The students agreed that Cerny knew his stuff: the punctuation, hyphenation, inter-punctuation, and underlying structure of the sentence, and the spacing of metaphors. But the students also agreed that the grammarian was sometimes laughed at for his incessant preaching and mentoring. When Ella told this to Lada, her friend chuckled without further comment. They understood each other, just from their eyes and the position of their eyebrows.

❈

"What does your American palate say to our Moravian vino?" Cerny asked.

"Very nice. Some acidity but when cooled down, well—my palate says good. But you know that the 'palate' is a fictional literary creation, Dr. Cerny. Taste buds are not in the palate but in the tongue and cheeks." She sniffed the wine.

"Your general knowledge, my dear, is admirable. But I have a great idea, too." Cerny leaned over the table with a forced grin, which made his face a landscape wrinkled by earthquakes. He put his hand on Ella's arm and slid it to over her hand. Ella froze, studying his moves.

"Well, instead of ordering another Moravian 'sun' we can drink something even more interesting." Cerny removed his hand slowly and covered his chin in a gesture of contemplation. "I can fix us the bestest martini this side of the river. What do you say, my friend?"

"What should I say?"

"Say, yes, great."

"Yes, great," Ella said, anticipating, correctly, the next suggestion.

"My apartment is about fifteen minutes away from the Slavia, just behind the Theatre," Cerny said. "All ingredients, and ice, are there, all at the ready!"

Ella saw a happy face, for the first time this afternoon. It wasn't the first time she had been invited to some suspicious apartment after a few drinks, but rarely was a dry martini used as a magnet. Mostly, she remembered, it was rum drinks.

Cerny paid and they were on their way. Ella had a last glimpse of Prague Castle above the river and gave a hail to *The Absinthe Drinker*, her most favorite painting in Prague. On the way Cerny offered her his arm, remarked on historical architecture, and praised the Goethe Institute as they passed. Indeed, it was not more than fifteen minutes later when they entered the apartment house.

Cerny seemed to have trouble opening the door of his flat. He pulled the key twice, mumbling. Ella observed his nervous lack of coordination and found it interesting. Then, gallantly, he held the door for her with an expansive motion of his arm. She liked the smell of the living room, the smell of antiquity and of leather, perhaps. She admired the writing table with its many tiny drawers, inlayed wood leaf with writing instruments, fountain pens, and an old-fashioned ink pot. She commented on the ancient almirah and scanned the books on the shelves covering one whole wall. A large coffee table with gray slate top was flanked by a well-used leather easy chair and modern, cheerful sofa. It all seemed to fit well in the bachelor-writer's pad. He walked rapidly to the corner desk with a turntable, radio and CD player. Ella, of course was well acquainted with the script, which goes as follows:

Step one. Music romantic, mellow.

Cerny put on a CD by Edith Piaf, "Je ne regrette rien". He turned to Ella with a big smile.

"Do you like this amazing *chansonniere*?"

"I do, Dr. Cerny, sad as she was."

Step two. Strong alcoholic beverage with aphrodisiacal side effect is served during the music.

The host opened a cabinet, which revealed a good selection of liquors and distillates.

"I promised you martini, arctic cold. So here you are," said the *charmeur* in a deeper-than-usual voice. Ella approached and watched the alchemist as he mixed gin and vermouth not 5:2 but 10:1—the killer, in Ella's book. He moved the shaker expertly, looking for her approval. Then he put olives in and a teaspoon of the olive brine. "This is called the 'dirty martini,' with the brine. It makes this black mamba's poison a little bit more mellow." He showed his dentures and offered the glass to Ella.

"*Na zdravi,* for health, as we say—and to my beautiful guest. This, Ella, is no parrot phrase—but you are special, my friend." He then talked about martinis. It seemed he was well educated, and described how Truman liked his martini, and how Eisenhower made them. She made some wily joke about gin and closed one eye.

Step three. Gradual undress.

"Can I?" He asked and slowly pulled her blouse up. She was thirty years old, a healthy Minnesota gal, so she'd had her six (seven?) romantic encounters, and she liked most of them, and she knew that life is chronologically short. But she didn't help him with his effort.

There were four very small hooks on the back of her bra, and Cerny worked hard. He managed to unhook only two, mumbling expletives which Ella did not understand, since she knew only '*hovno, prdel, sracka—to je nase znacka.*' Cerny grumbled some more and then gave up, with a short howl. He then kissed her. It was a humid kiss and he missed her mouth at first. He was forty-five years Ella's senior, the man from the generation of her grandparents—but he did not miss the second time.

Step four. The roll in the imaginary hay and union with riotous abandonment should follow.

Ella stood motionless as though watching a movie scene, and observed the man starting to take his pants off, giving her a sideways look, maybe a shrug of his narrow shoulders. He pulled one leg off the pants, but the other wouldn't go; it got tangled and Cerny fell, as if his legs were cut off from under him by machete. Ella looked on in amazement, since the fall appeared to her to be an exact copy, an animation of the most famous war photograph by Robert Capa, of a militiaman shot and falling in the Spanish civil war. The only difference was that Cerny did not hold a rifle but a martini glass, from which the two olives flew through the air in ballistic trajectory.

"My shoulder, oh, oh, my shoulder! Oh, oh." His moan was not in the usual cultivated baritone but was a child's cry—it was the confession of castrato. Ella rushed to help, to doctor this fallen Lothario, now helpless and in some pain. He moaned some more, then gave a short bark, which she took to be a laugh. She helped him to the sofa, and without comment, went to the cabinet, filled a shot glass with vodka, and pressed it to his hand. He looked diminished in the X-large black boxers, his spindly legs so white they seemed to emit fluorescence in the darkened room. As writers go, he was no Philip Roth—who swims a mile every day.

He gulped down the shot, whispered a short thanks, and lay there, breathing heavily. It appeared the evening's entertainments were at an end. Indecisive, and resisting an urge to run out, Ella grabbed her purse.

"Doctor Cerny, I think I should go now. But if you need any help, please, call me. And, pretty please, get X-rays tomorrow. It might be just the rotator cuff but one never knows." She did not thank him for the drink; it did not seem to be the right thing to say. He was in need of physical sympathy—but Ella just had to get out of there. At the door, with an uneasy feeling about her departure, she turned around and sent him an air-kiss, anyway. On the way home, she thought about a quote by Oscar Wilde, that the tragedy of growing old is that we remain young.

＊

It was a good morning for a run. Ella took the jogging-biking path along the river upstream from Palacky Square, about three miles, that day. The air was clear and bright, which made the bridges as sharp as Ansell Adams' prints of Yosemite's Half Dome, and the run a sheer pleasure. She greeted passing joggers the Minnesota way, but none answered. Only the beautiful swans on the stream, white like the summer cumulus, greeted her, honking their "Ahoy!" The river eluted a pleasant odor, in which Ella thought she detected a whiff of Pilsner Urquell, her favorite. It was a different perfume from the one she remembered rising from the Mississippi, up to West River Road, which she used to take to her alma mater. She missed it, now, the big river and its scent. She became a little homesick.

On the way home she stopped by Paukert Deli for six open face sandwiches to go, two with *malossol* caviar, which Lada would devour with sighs of pleasure. Lada would be coming for lunch and Ella would serve these *chlebicky* with Veltlin green wine, and they would gossip about writers, not writing. Ella planned to bring Cerny up. She was not sure if she would disclose her recent misadventure.

Lada arrived on time, as always, beaming with the pleasure of meeting a friend. She looked nice; she was tan (she rowed double skiff), her sun-bleached hair tied in a ponytail, swinging to accent her delight. The girls embraced and rushed to the table for the sandwiches and wine, like hungry savages, which they were. They raised glasses: "*Na zdravi*, to health, and to weirdos. Norwegian Nobels for both of us!"

"I had a lunch with Cerny, yesterday. We went to Slavia," Ella said.

"Whoa, did he feed and wine you well?"

"Yup, he was gentlemanly, for sure, but I was there for more than nourishment, Lada—I wanted to learn about him, a little, wanted to climb the circular star of his DNA, so to say, and also, to hear his opinion about Prucha's last novel…"

"I know what you're gonna say—he wanted to talk about his book, not Prucha's. Right?"

"You're right. It was embarrassing, a little. I learned nothing, but we managed, like civilized people, I think."

"And then he wanted to seduce you, to drag you into his lair." Lada laughed, watching her friend with eagle's eyes.

"How did you know that?"

"Hell, I know. I have survived in this city of Czech males all my life. Remember?" Lada said. "As a virgin!" She roared with a short laugh, amused by her fantasy.

"Have this *chlebicek* with caviar. I thought it was your favorite, since you returned from Paris," Ella said, to change the topic. "It ain't no result of molecular cooking with liquid nitrogen, as you'll see."

"Yes, thanks, it reminds me what those Parisian culinary sophisticates say. They claim that the greatest food France has offered to the world is morning-fresh baguette, sealed with village butter and piled with caviar. When washed down with Riesling cooled to seven centigrade—there is nothing better, ever," Lada swallowed, "and it's the bone-marrow truth, I can tell ya."

Lada raised her sandwich with both hands above eye level, as a Catholic priest would elevate the host in worship. And then with sounds of mastication and sipping of the Veltlin green, they both praised Paukert's creations.

"Coming back to Cerny," Ella said. "I read his last book and wanted to hear what do you think."

"Ella, dear, of course I'll tell, but you first. You are interested in what's going on in fiction writing in this country, more than I am."

Ella refilled the glasses and appeared to be lost in thought.

"Yeah, but besides my notion, that academia today is killing the fiction here, and everywhere, and Cerny is an academician, I can tell you that reading the most recent stuff, even in States—I just get desperate."

"You mean not only his work ?"

"Have you read any stories by Alice Munro, who won the Nobel? They're so boring they bring crocodile tears to my eyes. And Jhumpa Lahiri, who won the Pulitzer—her stories are all about Indian immigrants—those could be interesting only to East Indians and to the United States Immigration and Naturalization Service. All these should be *libri prohibiti*, if you ask me. And I am not even talking about the populist commercial trash." She shook her head.

"Aren't you too harsh today, my friend?" Lada asked, and pointed to the empty glass.

"I know, but sometimes I just ask, oh where, oh where are you, Somerset Maugham, old Ruski Nabokov, amazing

Polak Conrad, fisher Hemingstein, and I could go on and on. But let me first call Cerny, now, before I forget. He had some problem with his shoulder, and I want to find out what's going on."

Ella made a gesture as if stopping traffic, picked up her cell phone and dialed. She mouthed that nobody had picked up, just the voicemail.

"Hi Doctor Cerny, this is Ella; I wanted to know how you are and how your shoulder feels today. Just call me back, please, when you have a chance. Thank you, cheerio."

She put down the phone. "Back to his writing, Lada. I had it all summarized in brief: Cerny's scribbling is a classic example of bullshit without a story, without an interesting plot. He is a show-off with fancy language, with intentionally archaic expressions meant to impress, plenty of French quotations to be worldly, and nonsensical metaphors on every page. Verbosity, I can tell you, that …" suddenly Ella's face became ashen, her eyes bulged. Her hand came up as if surrendering, and then she grabbed the cell phone.

"Jesus! Oh my god! My god!" Ella howled, covered her face with her hands. "This is a catastrophe! I'm dead."

"What happened to you? What are you talking about?" Lada asked with anxiety in her voice, reaching for Ella's hand.

"It is a catastrophe! My phone was still on. Everything I just said is now in his goddamned voicemail!"

"Could you, please, recheck the phone?"

"It was on, Lada, it was on. See, 'last call 1 minute 30 seconds.' I'm gonna die, girlfriend!"

Ella could only emit onomatopoetic sounds of despair; Lada could only hold her hand. They sat in silence till Lada came up with an idea to break into Cerny's voicemail and erase the message. But for such a deed of desperation one would, at least, need the voicemail number and password. It was just a fantasy.

"I am skunked, my friend, I am hosed," Ella whispered, and slumped into a chair in the fetal position, like a refuse heap of calamities.

"Well, Ella, you are going to leave this city in a few days, and you'll leave behind everything, even your sins," Lada attempted a grin. "Maybe the best thing to do is to just to focus on packing all your stuff, and to think about the 'Land of 10,000 Lakes,' your home. It has been written in books of wisdom, that time takes care of everything. Almost everything." Lada hugged her friend and wiped her tears with her sleeve. "So they say."

And so it happened. Ella packed and left on a jet plane.

❇

Back home Ella settled into her old apartment by the river, finished her thesis and got a degree with distinction. She jogged along West River Road above the mighty Misi-Ziibi, her old—and new—love. But first thing every morning she would get on the Internet and check the Czech website www.lidovky.cz for the news. In the Obituaries column, she had found nothing disturbing, yet. Then after about a year, in the *Kultura* section, she read that Professor Cerny had become a finalist in the prestigious Magnet Litera Literary Prize, which Czech literati more or less award to themselves.

He was lauded for his excellence in storytelling and for lifetime literary achievements. So, Ella could sleep a full eight hours now without being troubled by recurring nightmares.

She sent out fifteen job applications to publishing companies, newspapers, and literary magazines, and was able to live in hope. Meanwhile, she got a job with Yellow Taxi and successfully competed with Somali Islamists, who would not take passengers with dogs or carrying booze from the duty-free shops.

In her free time she would sit ruminating by the window, through which she tried to see, in vain, the river with the white swans that greeted her with "Ahoy," and the enchanted Castle above. She left the window the day she started to write. Her first creation was the short story titled "The Cell Phone Incident".

Tegucigalpa

Danny was a traveler known for his preference for suffering. He felt exhilaration amid the botanical density of a misty rain forest, at 90% humidity and wild Fahrenheits. A prerequisite for his happiness was the presence of wild native hominoids; he liked different peoples but preferred to be near savages distant to the savage culture from which he had originated. This time, though, he'd arrived in a city where there were no botanical wonders. The city was known for its inhabitants' tendency to commit violence. It was a town anybody would be terrified to be near, especially at night. He'd landed in Tegucigalpa, the capital of Honduras, the original Banana Republic.

Before the trip Danny had to decide which of the Central American countries to explore. He'd visited the great bookstore Barnes & Noble and found the travel section. There he checked the six-foot long row of travel guides for Central America and noted that the only country missing was Honduras. No eager tourists or vacationers seemed to be interested in it. The decision to buy a round trip ticket from American Airlines was thus made easily. The decision by the local rulers to drive away United Fruit and Chiquita from their banana republic resulted in the reversion of the country to its initial state of primitive existence and poverty, and thus was a promising new territory for Danny to explore.

Landing in Tegucigalpa airport was interesting, since the landing gear nearly clipped the palm thatch and corrugated iron roofs of the shacks of a local favela (slum). The plane's brakes had to be applied vigorously on the short runway, their screams accompanied by applause from passengers with sweaty temples and eyes wide in fear. Danny got his duffel bag and dragged it to the nearby road to flag down a taxi for less than half the price of those picking up passengers in front of the airport entrance. He registered in an inexpensive dormitory-hotel near the main square and got a thick boiled coffee from the concierge, who instructed him to be "very careful on the street, bad characters are there waiting for a gringo." Then he collapsed on his cot under a mosquito net, the gossamer symbol of the adventurous tropics, falling asleep with a smile on his face.

❄

The nearby square, Plaza de San Isidro, when lighted by the noon sun, is a stage for an unending opera buffa. When Danny entered the curtain was up—a chorus of vendors of known and unknown tropical fruits in half-sold carts lifted their arms in animated barter, actors playing decrepit beggars on the church's stairs slowed their begging, a group of old men gathered around a domino game slapped down pieces as if each one was a victory, a pod of young delinquents with weird hairdos observed the stranger with sideways glances, and uniformed men with submachine guns standing at each of the four corners of the square smoked. Danny found a place on a bench next to a senior mestizo who cradled a black puppy.

As puppy-dogs are reliable starters of conversation among all people of the world except Muslims, Danny started in with "Nice doggie, how old is the pup?"

The man smiled; he expected the question. "Three months, señor. Still fresh." He kissed the little beast.

"You are a happy man, having such a fluffy, faithful friend."

Strangers in Latin America do not talk much about stock market or globalization, so the two talked about the economy of the country in the most simple terms: robberies.

"But, *mi amigo*, you have to be very alert walking the streets of our city. Dangerous people are hiding there. They kill."

"Strange you say that. I walked a little through the old town and there was peace everywhere," Danny said.

"Your eyes are not focused well, señor. This could bring you grief. *Assassinos* do not advertise, you see?"

"Are there parts of the city I should avoid?"

"At night it is dangerous, *muy pericoloso*, everywhere. Maybe around the market the darkness is deadliest. In the evening the solitary *malignos* are like sharks, but when night falls they come in schools like piranhas. There is no escape, then, señor."

Danny had a nice dinner in a bodega next to his hotel, rice and beans with pulled pork which he chased down with imported Pilsner Urquell at the near perfect temperature. Sleep under the mosquito net came lightning-fast.

✳

Next day, disguised as a tourist and mimicking a gringo, Danny visited a farm for green iguanas (which only served to remind him how cruelly animals were treated by Latinos), rummaged through an antique store with looted Aztec artifacts, and admired the skill of tobacco rollers in the manufacture of famous Honduran cigars. After drinking a mojito and smoking the same famous Honduran cigar in his hotel, he changed his t-shirt and started in the direction of the Bar Litera, where, supposedly, the local literati gathered. He was warned again not to wander farther than two blocks: *dos cuadras no delante atras, por favor.* On the city plan it looked not farther than a fifteen-minute walk, maybe.

In the bar he was not visible. A few older men drank greenish fluid, talked fast, and when Danny approached with a smile, regarded him as a stranger, an uninvited intruder into a conversation between old friends. So Danny had a lonely dinner, including a few mojitos. He paid the monoligual waiter and left. Night had descended on Tegucigalpa.

The only living creature on the street was a midsize dog with a submissive gaze and a limp. There was no other option than to walk; he knew the way. He knew the danger, too, as he had been warned repeatedly, and the gunshots in the distance, cutting through the silence, confirmed. He was still alone when he passed the locked gate of the market. The beggars had disappeared with the light, and rats scurried away at his sight. When Danny saw five men in the distance fear flooded his consciousness.

There are several parts of the brain where fear has its home. The amygdala of emotions, the anterior cingulate, and the prelimbic cortex have regions which would light up on functional magnetic resonance imaging if the patient were frightened. Many of those four trillion connections would spread our fear around the brain, making it a rapid but complex feeling. In *Homo sapiens* the prefrontal cortex can often deal with emotions by applying reason. The feeling of fear could thus be either critically useful—or paralyzing and thus deadly. Simple.

Danny did not freeze but continued walking, his anxiety not showing, his pace as regular and unhurried as he could control. The five young men silently approached and surrounded him, so he had to stop. He managed his expressions as much as possible, trying to show disinterest, which came out as a submissive grin, anyway. Inside he was sad. He realized too well that these moments might be the last moments of his consciousness, and possibly, of his life. He could not read the expressions of the young men. Their faces were those of mestizos, Indian-white half-breeds; they were small in stature, their movements fluid and not hurried, showing that they belonged in the urban jungle as a wild beast belongs in a rain forest. They showed the confidence of their collective power. They hunted at night, which was their friend. They gazed at Danny with surprise, and started to talk between themselves using short sentences and utterances. Danny's hands sweated, his legs felt feeble, as expected, as they should. He did not move.

The tall one with a baseball bat and cap, pushed one of his companions forward, the one with an uncertain smile drawn by a scar on the lip.

"Señor gringo, you can not be in night," he said in English. "You in danger in night here. Go home! Rapido!" He approached Danny and pushed him quite gently. Danny started walking, followed by the toughies, who laughed and chatted in a lingo he did not understand. They followed him all the way to his hotel, and then disappeared, like translucent spirits of the dark night, without a sound.

Danny sat down on the stairs breathing regularly, shaking his head in equal intervals. He was alive.

Tanks and Quantum Mechanics in 1968

That morning in August was the grayest morning anyone had seen, with the sky so lead-heavy it sank low enough to touch the spires of the ancient, gingerbread city of Prague. But people would not recall the sky; all they would remember would be the tanks.

For Mirek it all started at five in the morning when the doorbell rang. No one rings the doorbell at five, so everyone in the family got up—Mirek, his father, mother, even his grandmother descended in her historical nightgown. Mother opened the door to find Mrs. Mori standing there with an expression barely recognizable. (Mrs. Mori was a classy, cultured Jewish lady, the next-door neighbor, who married Susumu Mori, the Japanese scientist, whom she left. Then she married Hirsch, who left her, so she was living alone.)

"Mrs. Mori, Mrs. Mori," Mirek's mother said, "can we be of some help?" It was a moment of anxiety, since Mori seemed to have lost her lung power for a while.

"The Russians invaded, the Mongol hoards are here!" she raised her voice. "The Mongol hoards are here," she whispered, then stood there as if paralyzed a moment, before shuffling back to her apartment across the hall, bent like a weeping willow in a flurry. All the family gathered in the kitchen.

"Hon, should I call Peter?" Mother broke the silence. (Professor Peter Zvolen was a famous psychiatrist, and the family's close friend.) "It's pretty early, but Mrs. Mori might have … something is wrong with her head, she looked so … disturbed, talking nonsense."

"Wait, let me check the radio—I know she might be getting mad but one never knows…" Father said and lit a cigarette, his earliest ever.

Mirek went to the window and when he opened it, the living room was instantly filled with a deep rumble resembling the echo of distant thunder. However, this thunder was accompanied by a metallic staccato. The family gathered by the windows. Thalman Street offered a scene from a war movie, a sight which everybody, at first, considered a delusion. Like gray iron horseshoe crabs, tanks and transporters were slowly moving in formation as far as one could see. The mirage was cloaked in exhaust fumes, the scent of which had not been inhaled before. The only colors on the street were the red stars painted on the sides of the vehicles and tanks.

Mirek dug into his meager word supply: "Holy shit, holy shit!" He repeated, rapidly combing his hair with his fingers. Father, meanwhile, confirmed the catastrophe with news from the radio, which called for the citizens to remain calm. Mother sat down by the kitchen table with Grandmother. Grandma had been a down-to-earth lady in any situation; she had a Victorian streak of toughness from living through two World Wars, under the rule of Nazis, then Communists. It had been traded among the extended family that nobody had ever seen her cry. Now she held her gray head in her hands and thinly wailed. That view shook Mirek as much as seeing the tanks. This was the most wretched morning in the world.

The day was spent mostly listening to the radio. On the telephone Father organized a meeting of his friends in the apartment. The earliest rumors were that Czechoslovakia might become one of the Soviet republics. Even if this prospect was widely believed to be in the realm of fantasy, it was certain that in the future the country would become an even tougher communist dictatorship than before. Walking the street, as masses of wide-eyed citizens did, it was clear that the Prague Spring was over.

The next day Father's friends gathered in the apartment. They were all lettered men of education, readers, men to be trusted to respond properly to a change of environment, which is one of the definitions of IQ. There were seven of them, and they called themselves "The Magnificent Seven" (to the riotous amusement of their wives). Father used to say these were men of solid character, of honor, and wit, who would never join the Party, who one could trust, always, loyal friends, who knew plenty of jokes and stories, too. They used to meet once a month, in secret, since it was against the law for more than three to gather without special permission by the Party enforcers. They had known each other for ages. Mirek admired his father for having friends like that; one must be special to have friends like The Magnificent Seven.

❅

Mirek was a second year student in the Department of Mathematics and Physics at the University. He had good physical development not unusual for his eighteen years, attesting to his diligent efforts at hockey in winter and tennis for the rest of the year. Five feet eight, a few pimples, long hair. But the development of his mind, particularly the part involved with mathematics, was preternaturally advanced—he was a veritable wunderkind. It was a matter of genetics, the result of a series of accidental mutations, perhaps. Still, he was well liked by his peers because he was always helpful, and, mostly, because it was obvious he valued his minor achievements in hockey as far more important that his amazing ability in math.

At home things had been good. Mirek loved his mom and liked his father, except when Dad beat him in tennis. Their relationship was almost always based on reason. Reason was big in the family but emotions were still encouraged as often as one would add important spices to the humble Szegedin goulash. Mirek treated Grandma with some respect; he liked her as a giver of presents, a nice relict from a distant planet. Sometimes it helped that she was hard of hearing and had cataracts.

So he lived the life of a fairly happy young man, strictly avoiding matters of politics. He kept himself ignorant of the details of Party schemes in school. It was his Kevlar shield, the math and physics, protecting him, like a Zulu's shield of hippo hide, from the spears and arrows of intrigues formed by the bad characters around him. Even as teenagers some of his mates, toadies, profiteers, had joined the Communist Youth to benefit themselves.

Mirek's existence had been punctuated with only minor excitement, till he spilled his white coffee on the miniskirt of his schoolmate Irene, in the Department's cafeteria. She let him wipe the skirt and that was the first time he touched her.

He apologized like a madman, and she told him his hands trembled like someone with Parkinson's, but as a matter of statistical probability it should not happen again. Then they talked.

Irene was one of the rare few females in Physics. She was considered a "smart blonde," so smart that her male schoolmates were scared of her; in their testosterone haze they preferred "dumb blondes." Besides, she liked cosmology and astrophysics, the more bizarrely incomprehensible of physics' branches. Mirek noticed her the first day of school; he watched her with secret wishes, but never approached. In his eyes she was pretty like a picture and her occasional display of genius in seminars made her even more beautiful to him. He loved to watch from a safe distance her lovely skin, her fine features, her slick volleyball body, and the gray cat-like eyes in her heart-shaped face, not always ready for a smile.

They started to date. She was ashamed, at first, of her virginity so she faked experience in body and mind, too. It worked well for both of them. The few weeks before the Soviet invasion was a golden time for Mirek and Irene; it had nothing to do with the reality surrounding them.

This rapid romance of sex-suppressed juveniles was followed by an unexpected friendship, which seemed like the most important thing in the world, changing their lives. Their constant problem was to find a place. Hotels were out of the question due to their lack of cash. Irene lived with her mother who rarely left the apartment, and in Mirek's apartment Grandmother watched like the multi-headed dog Cerberus guarding the Underworld. Their only refuge was their good friend Jirka's pad, which was to be had, sometimes, till about 10 PM at the latest. And there, in Jirka's bed, they hurried sex and hurried drinking cheap Bulgarian red, to make it by ten. They also talked. They loved to joke about physics. Mirek worried about what would happen when supercomputers became smarter than humans, while Irene swore that the cosmological constant must be some kind of weird dark matter.

"If you worry at all, my sexual technologist," Irene laughed, "then worry about understanding asymmetric quantum mechanics." She tried to sound serious. "How the hell can the electron be in two places at the same time?"

"Hey, I love your symmetry, though, if you know what I mean!" He kissed her closemouthed. "It makes me cross-eyed, I swear."

"Mirek, I am not joking! If I could understand just the principle, then you'd have a famous girlfriend. Then, maybe, I could understand the goddamned fourth spatial dimension in the parallel Universe. Or what?"

"It will all come, my Irene. Worry not," Mirek assured her.

"Yeah, and what about that tiny bitch Singularity? What does it do in those gigantic black holes, and why does she, the bitch, allow not even light to escape her event horizon?" Irene whispered. Jirka, their good friend and Great Benefactor, was coming soon to claim his mattress of sins, so they had to hurry their copulatory training and, this time, Hungarian Egri Bikavér, "bull's blood" red wine, the rare delicacy. That would have to be all for tonight—the night of affection was over. They lacked no tenderness, but time was after them like leopard after an agouti.

Irene was dressing up, and couldn't find her panties (she always lost her panties) but she was still going on: "One more thing. I just can't figure out: how that young Indian Chandrasekhar, from the land where they have castes, untouchables and no toilets, could calculate his Chandrasekhar limit with such … elegance. Tell me!"

Mirek finished the last drop of the red wine. "I think it is no different than when my beautiful genius Irene will figure out the magnetism of the Singularity—while coming from the Czech University rated as low as three hundredth in the world. No difference. Ha!" They heard Jirka unlocking the door.

❄

It happened three days before the invasion. Irene arrived with a radiant face. After their lovemaking they rested, breathing deeply, with sweat on Mirek's brow.

"I have for you two big items of news, great news, boyo!" She grinned in expectation of Mirek's scream. "First is that I figured out one of the principles of the Singularity, the miniscule shit which gave rise to everything." Mirek sat up, faking amazement and understanding.

Irene said: "It is like our mutual orgasm, you know, where time has no past and no future and no laws of physics apply, not even quantum mechanics. How about that?"

"Perfect, Irene, perfect!"

"And the second great item of news, wait for that, is that my ma decided to go to Lustige Zwitchenbrucke, Veselé Meziříčí, in South Bohemia for vacation. She'll be gone for a week, starting tomorrow!"

Mirek screeched a hoot of disbelief. He thought that Irene's brain must be twice life-sized and there was a cozy place there for him. Love.

"We'll have the place to ourselves," Mirek lowered his voice. "It is unbelievably smashing, wicked, fan-fucking-tastic, fantabulous ... my gal!" He beamed. He would realize his secret dream—that they would make love any time, for lunch, maybe, just any time. But the biggest part of his dream, which he had sheltered and hid, which he did not share, was that they would make breakfast together. They would put on music, Handel or Elvis, she topless, he in his Mickey Mouse pajama pants, just like married people! (He thought.) Yeah, he would make eggs, any way Irene wanted, he could do it. They'd rub shoulders and butts in the kitchen and laugh. This dream would come true in a couple of days. And they would bullshit about anything, anything stupid like string theory, the existence of black holes or Higgs particles. They would talk seriously, frivolously, bawdily. Alone, just two of them.

❄

When Mirek spied the war machines that fateful morning, he realized that besides the country's tragedy, his dream with Irene might just remain in the goddamned realm of dreams. Irene did not have a working telephone, so the only way to reach her was to go to her house in Zahradni Street. So he changed and was on the way, sneaking between the tanks standing in front of their apartment. The tanks and armored personnel carriers were parked, not moving at all now, as if to stay forever, on all the bridges over the Vltava River, on ancient squares, on the streets. There were bullet holes on the walls of the National Museum, some apartment houses, and City Hall, so Mirek could see that there must have been at least some resistance to the burial of hopes. But there were no real battles, since the Soviet power was so overwhelming that any risks would be self-defeating and would result in a greater tragedy. Besides, the fighting spirit has not been encoded in the autosomal chromosomes of Bohemians, as displayed in history with rare exceptions when preservation of property, and sometimes lives, prevailed.

Walking, Mirek saw citizens reasoning and arguing with the inhabitants of the Soviet war vehicles and tanks in Czech and Russian; some stumbled around like in a funeral procession, some screamed obscenities at the occupiers. But the responses of soldiers were mostly blank stares, or rare utterances explaining that "they arrived to defeat the armed rebellion against peoples and socialism." They did not hurrah as they were taught, and a few of the soldiers, those of simple features, apparently thought they were in Russia, still. Their faces, Caucasian and Asian, hung down in fatigue and confusion. A Siberian Buryat, with an expression of cognitive impairment, sitting on the turret of the megalithic Land Battleship T-35, announced to open-mouthed Pragers that this place was West Germany. A deep-bosomed matron shrieked at him an obscenity in high C. A dark-jowled man spat on the tank runners. *Job tvoju mat*, he announced his plan regarding the occupant's mother. But there were no fights.

Mirek felt the urge to contribute, at least with a threatening gesture, or scream, but all he could do was to shake his head. At the end of the bridge he observed an older lady who raised her tiny fist—but remained mute, silently crying. Fragile was the fist of the old woman now and the tears on her cheeks were salty, as salty as before, during the previous occupation of her land. Shaken by the lament of the grandma, he bent his head and dragged himself in the direction of Marx Square, from which Irene's Zahradni Street started.

At the mouth of the street he joined a crowd of people who were mingling around and talking excitedly. Nobody could enter the street, since a line of Russian soldiers blocked them. These were very different soldiers than those on the war machines. They were dressed in clean uniforms free of insignia or other identifications, their red berets were a color variation of the American Green Berets, and they wore them without a frivolous slant. They did not carry automatic weapons, only side arms which they had holstered. The most unusual thing about these specialists were their calm faces—these were faces with features of intelligence. They did not show fatigue or confusion; the men wore expressions of confidence. They did not communicate with the crowd, nor did they respond to any questions. In the eyes of the specialists the individuals in the crowd did not exist. None of the people of the crowd screamed at them; they were silent.

"What is happening, sir?" Mirek asked an older man.

"These creatures are guarding the street, because a block from here, there is the Central Committee Secretariat of the Party. You should know that." The man paused. "And there, my man, the traitors, our famous Bolsheviks, there they are waiting for orders from Moscow," the man continued, more for himself than for Mirek. "During the German occupation, their SS Schutzstaffel officers looked exactly like these cool killers. I remember well the sunovabiches…"

Mirek could not proceed into Zahradni Street. He turned back home, bent in utter despair. He felt like death. He bumped into people. At home he locked himself in his cubicle. Not even an experienced psychologist would be able to understand the turmoil in his mind, the sudden state of nerves, the mind devoid of all dreams so suddenly.

That evening, the third day after the invasion, Father's friends, the Magnificent Seven, gathered in the living room. The long table was covered with cigarette packs, ashtrays, shot glasses with slivovice, Becher liquor, and Cuban Bacardi, as after a merry celebration. The alcoholic beverages, this time, did not elevate the mood, since the men gathered to discuss emigration. The conclusions which would be reached would not be not a collective decision, but each one of the group would try to clarify his thoughts. As they all knew, their decisions, after consulting with their better halves, would be of gravest consequence for them and their family.

Calmly, six of the seven presented their thoughts for and against. Only one of them, no isolato otherwise, to be sure, did not consider the possibility of leaving the country, without clarifying his reasons, which were hidden in the mega-compartment for secrets in his calvarium. The most prevailing argument for leaving the country, which was agreed upon by all, concerned the future of their kids or the future of their future progeny. They refused to bring up the children in the character-bending prison of the dictatorship. So, they would join 100,000 other beer specialists, mushroom collectors, skiers, dumpling eaters and atheists—refugees, freedom seekers.

Within a week of the meeting, six of the Magnificent Seven would leave the country for France, Germany, Switzerland, and that America of dreams. Their voyages westward could be written as short stories, adventurous and interesting—interesting being the highest praise for a work of non-fiction, and fiction, as well.

❊

Next morning, after the meeting, Mirek was called from his refuge-cubicle to the kitchen table and there it was announced that in two days the family, including Grandma, would pack a few things into their Fiat 850 and leave for Holland, where Dad had friends, and from there to America, where he had other friends. It had to be done rapidly, before the borders became hermetically sealed, as they had been for the past twenty years. They would leave behind everything, everybody, their previous lives, looking for a refuge from their present existence.

Father said: "It is possible to change life and to find happiness—even greater than before." He took some time to look at the faces of his family. "We'll do it. Together!"" Since Father never used big words and never subscribed to philosophies, everybody around the kitchen table would remember his words.

But what happened to Irene? Will Mirek need a prefrontal lobotomy to cut Irene from his mind?

Cognitive archeology teaches us that through hominoid evolution the human brain has been conditioned to survive stress by action. And so it happened: the car was washed, prepared for the journey, and a few of the most nostalgic of heirloom possessions and important documents were loaded. In these confused hours of departure, Mirek, now a juvenile refugee to be, smuggled in his graphite Head Graphen XT tennis racket, which he hid under the front seat.

This story must end abruptly—as suddenly as the anomalous lives and hopes of Mirek's family and friends ended. That morning the sky mutated from gray to incandescent forget-me-not blue, but nobody noticed, meteorology did not matter. All that expired after the Fiat 850 left the Thalman Street westward is now a matter of record.

Excursion to the Land of the Jesus Christ Lizard

Today I left behind the beautiful city of Medellin, the domain of the cocaine lord Pablo Escobar—therefore, the murder capital (25/week) of Colombia. We departed from the municipal airport downtown, which is served by the small local Aces Airlines. The baggage handler took my Eddie Bauer duffel bag and on this pleasant sunny morning I crossed the tarmac with about twenty other passengers, half of them black, since our destination was Quibdó, a town in the remote Choco district, which is inhabited mostly by descendants of runaway Negro slaves.

Crossing the tarmac to a plane often changes something in me; I am filled with strange elation. Maybe it is the feeling of impending freedom, maybe the anticipation of an exotic adventure which makes my legs lift higher and my palms sweat, as I move with an imbecilic grin on my face, my inner landscape flooded by sunlight. Before I climbed the stairs of the plane I motioned to the airline employee to approach.

"How safe are Aces aeroplanes, señor?" I asked half in jest. The older man, wearing an incomplete uniform and with features of a Cholo Indian, looked at me in surprise, raising his eyebrows.

"*Seguro, señor, seguro*" he nodded.

"I mean do they fall?"

"*No, señor, no accustombrado.*" Not usually, he assured me, and walked away.

Feeling better now, suspecting our plane might not crash *normalmente*, I found my place by the window. Next to me sat an older lady with an appearance of high class. Perhaps from the coffee growers' clans, she would be addressed as *Doña*, I surmised. We did not exchange any small talk. She seemed to be confused by the seat belts, but, finally, managed. We exchanged a formal nod.

The departure of our plane, powered by two propellers, was delayed only an hour, which I knew was not excessive, considering the ways of South American organization and lifestyle. We took off well, flying first across the *precordillera*, then through the mighty Andes.

The *precordilliera* was composed of green hills and brown streams snaking through valleys, some winding through clumps of shacks; one could see coffee plantations and horsemen in groups. The flight was peaceful, and I enjoyed the view. After about half an hour the hills grew higher and higher and the plane continued its steep climb. The landscape changed dramatically and it appeared we would not fly over and above the jagged peaks, some covered with snow. Not far from my window I could see a vertical wall. Then another. Then we penetrated a cumulus cloud and emerged close to the vertical rocky precipice. This may be a delight for mountaineers and boulderers, but we were so close that I could recognize the genus of orchids hanging from the crevice as dendrobiums. Another cloud, another miss and the lady next to me took my hand without giving me a look, her grip surprisingly firm, octopus-like. The plane started a slow descent. She did not release me till our successful landing.

Beneath us the vast jungle announced we were past the Andes. As far as one could see there was the rain forest, the vegetable wilderness of my desires, looking like tightly packed clubs of broccoli, extending from horizon to horizon. When we approached the landing strip a flock of ravens took flight. We touched down and all the passengers applauded, exuberance in their eyes, and hysterical yodels were heard. The lady next to me released my hand with many *gracias* and gave me a smile, saying something I did not understand. When the door of plane opened, the humid air dashed in and fogged over all the windows in an instant. Then everybody rushed out in feverish emergency, as if every second counted. I was the last one out, ablaze in the sunlight.

On the tarmac, passengers sprinted to get to their friends' motorcycle, moped, bike or car, and were gone. Just me and Eddie stood there in front of the shack-like "terminal," breathing deeply. The smoke from outdoor kitchens, whiffs of rotten vegetables, humid scents of botany, all tied together by the indescribable smell of the cracked laterite soil, which seemed to unite the odors together like the spermaceti of sperm whale stabilizes the mix of the most luxurious perfumes. It was an olfactory feast, and it raised my heartbeat to a gallop and corners of my lips sky-high.

Then, suddenly, *deus ex machina*, a Jeep arrived, spray-painted pink, with a roof of flapping, translucent polyethylene; it stopped just a foot from me. The driver motioned me to get in. His faced had absorbed so many photons it was as black as the cosmic black hole—I could see only his radiant eyes with yellow whites. I tossed in my Eddie Bauer and we were on our way—till a mile further on, where we got a flat. I howled in despair, guessing it would be an hour's delay.

"No señor, once minutas." Eleven minutes, he said, as if amused. And he was right. In twenty minutes we were passing the smoldering garbage dump and entering the town of Quibdó on Avenida d'Oro. My second visit there. The Jeep came to a slow stop in front of my "hotel," just a block from Calle Kennedy, where young mothers, part time prostitutes, gather after sundown for business and social intercourse. I paid the driver almost all he asked, offered him a cigarette (he took three) and entered the Hotel Intercontinental. It was a two story wooden structure with the facade decorated by multicolored tropical fungi and lichens; from its roof ferns waved at me. Inside I woke up the concierge from a deep sleep. She raised her head and gave me a surprised smile. She was beautiful, which is not an uncommon result of Negro-Caucasian-Indian triracial outbreeding. Her dark eyes were especially attractive in a smile, from their slight Mongolian slant, and her upper lip was beautifully succulent (without a Botox injection, I was sure). She gave me the key for a second floor room saying with a shy smile: *"Señor, muy bella vista!"* And soon I found she was right about the view—a view over the vastness of the Rio Atrato.

The room looked clean and only a few gigantic, honey-colored cockroaches scurried in panic to their secret hideaways, leaving me alone. There was a small table with a chair, shower corner, washbasin stand, and a bed domed by a mosquito net. A naked light bulb was sparkling with interesting insects. There are a few basic rules for traveling in tropics; one of the first order is to inspect the mosquito net for holes and tears. Mine was perfect. The most wonderful discovery was a spacious balcony hanging above the river. I did not hesitate and sank into the wicker chair by the balcony's railing. The sun was about to dive behind the jungle across the stream, dividing the river in parallel stripes of black asphalt and blinding silver ribbon. A few flocks of parrots passed by on their way to their night perch, and I opened my flat flask with local Aquardiente, anisette-flavored poison, which in this milieu tasted not glorious, but good. The shot and my Benson and Hedges cigarette induced in me a very special feeling, an elation hard to describe and even harder to understand. I had arrived; I did not think.

A few large sphinx moths and night butterflies on the wall stretched their wings for takeoff, disregarding the waiting acrobatic bats. I watched gecko lizards hunting the succulent insects on the ceiling, scurrying effortlessly upside down, alternating a motionless stand with the lightning fast dash for a hit. Their eyes could rotate 180 degrees in their sockets. There were no night-biting mosquitoes, yet.

It was dark when I descended to the street and soon found an eatery with covered veranda on the street level, called Boringen. After downing another Aquardiente "Platino" to dissolve my mucus, and to keep my mood elevated, I ordered chicken with beans and rice, the usual staple. It tasted excellent since the local poultry feeds on beetles, caterpillars, earwigs, spiders, lizards and anoles.

From the speakers hanging just above me, local tunes, the deadly salsa, blasted full volume, but it did not change my sunny disposition. The moronic repeats of *"amor," "mi corazon," "passion," "te quiero"* and *"dolor,"* while they would usually be a royal dolor in my behind, sounded almost like a lullaby, and I raised the mug with a pint of cold brew (the true *eaux de vie,* water of life, if there ever was one) to greet passing-by citizens, who stared at the white stranger with half open mouths and uncertain smiles.

❊

After a breakfast of banana, mango, and coffee, I loaded a small backpack with a can of sardines, two bananas, a killing jar for collecting beetles (I collect mainly jewel beetles, genus *Buprestidae*), an Opinel knife for cutting philodendrons (there are possibly some undescribed species, here in Choco) and a small dish towel and plastic bottle with water (commercial, NOT from the tap). I put on an oversized t-shirt, shorts without underwear and Merrell sandals.

One can enter the forest from the river, but then a prudent traveler should engage a local guide, so as not to become lost. Another way to enter the jungle is by following a creek, which trickles out of the forest. This has been my preferred way, if only because the Choco streams do not contain piranhas, electric eels, dangerous stingrays or parasitic schistosomiasis. The only dangers one might encounter would be a jaguar and two species of poisonous snakes, none of which likes water, anyway. The deadly poisonous "dart frog" is harmless unless its venom enters the bloodstream; it could safely be petted. So, the creek is a comfortable, safe route into the forest of tangled roots, thickets of ferns, impenetrable clumps of bamboo, vortices and knots of vines and lianas, and tentacles of rattan (some decorated with blossoms like traffic lights in the green darkness), between giant trees with buttresses, strange palms with thorns, some without a trunk, some with aerial roots, *renako*, *ceiba*, ironwoods, mahogany, gumbo-limbo trees, and hundreds of other species ... all spreading, reproducing, dying, blooming in an indefatigable riot of Nature, while a nice sandy stream silently winds through it all, with me.

I caught the rickety bus going to the outpost of Ithmina, upstream. The driver was an old black man who reminded me of my uncle—and, there again, I wondered how all very old men and women resemble each other regardless of their race or ethnicity, their racial features erased by the ravages of senility. He promised to let me out at the first crossing over the creek, a tributary of the Atrato. I remembered there was a bridge over the stream not too far from Quibdó. I thanked him profusely and got out there. Underneath I saw two grandmothers panning for gold. They used their *bateas* with the movements of experienced gold washers.

Bateas are shallow wooden dishes about two feet wide, often beautiful objects, since the tropical hardwood is of deep brown or brick color and the craftsmen who fashion them are concerned not only with its the function but also the pattern of wood grain, which they carve symmetrically, just to please the eye. One of the grandmothers laughed, showing her companion a yellow "tail" in the dish. It would feed her grandchildren for at least a day, I thought. When descending to the creek I greeted the women, but they turned away. A stranger is not to be trusted.

Soon after I started to wade upstream the creek became pleasantly clear, its size and depth perfect, the sandy bottom easy to wade in my sandals. I wanted to sing, entering the "green hell", *L'enfer vert*, which it wasn't, being a botanical garden without the entrance fee (only the exit is not always guaranteed) with many pleasant surprises. The first surprise I encountered just after one wide bend was when from under the elephant leaves of a plant a foot-and-a-half long a creature blasted out. It was the amazing Basilisc lizard (*Basiliscus basiliscus*). She dashed up the creek, in full speed, running on the surface, her legs slapping the water with the pace of a rock drummer, till she disappeared, dove under. I'd witnessed a miracle, I thought.

This creature has been called the Jesus Christ Lizard, since it has been traded, that in analogy, Jesus, the fabled preacher man from suburban Nazareth, also walked on the water (Mathew 14:22-24). However, I could not see even a comparison with my Basilisk, since J. Christ could not have dived—he was no diver.

I rested a while, ate a banana, got a sip of water, and then continued with intermittent wading and hiking on the sandy shore. Strange sounds from the forest were constant companions, but as it is the rain forest, one hears but does not see. In some places I had to deviate into the forest, because the bank was too narrow, or steep, or the stream had a drop-off and became too deep. In one of these short forest treks I stopped when I heard strange sounds. It was not the bark of monkeys, but human voices coming from the creek. In a few seconds, through a clump of bamboo, I spied them. There were three men, standing in the water working with *bateas*;

two more were taking a smoke break on the shore. These were *garimpeiros*, as they are known in Brazil, gold washers, a hard lot, secretive and dangerous when jealous and protecting their hidden claims, their *minas de oro*.

A lot has been written about fear, but one aspect of dread repeatedly reconfirmed is that in the proper dose fear can save your life. I had to decide what to do. Should I approach with a wide smile, or run? In hindsight none of the decisions would have guaranteed my safety. I slowly, very stealthily crawled back between the tangled vegetation. My naked arm touched the trunk of a palm with thorns and I emitted a sound. The *garimpeiros* froze as one and, instantly, the two men on smoke break dashed in my direction. I started to run and in a few moments, through the thicket of ferns, I emerged on the creek's bank, where I could move with increased speed. I looked back and saw that the one with cigarette on his lips had given up, and the younger one, without a shirt and in pants held by a rope around his waist, had started to gain on me. When I passed a sharp bend in the creek I heard behind me a scream and a flood of sounds which I took as obscenities. The man was emerging from the drop-off he did not know about, which I had bypassed; only his head showed. The chase was over. I could slow down.

When I returned to the bridge my wobbly legs ordered me to sit down and rest. The gold panning grandmothers were gone, for nobody in the tropics works overtime. I measured my heartbeat—it was 80 and descending. The chase must have lasted just three or four minutes, but I couldn't know exactly, since time for a speeding objects dilates, and changes with the object's increasing speed (Einstein: $E=mc^2$).

After climbing up to the road I started in the direction of Quibdó. At about the half way mark the ancient bus driver picked me up and insisted on taking me to the front of my hotel, disregarding the protests of other passengers. I had made a new friend.

After a short cold shower I changed my t-shirt and went for dinner. Downstairs, my favorite concierge (her name is Ignacia) cracked me a nice smile; we chatted a little. She wore an off-white blouse with décolletage so deep it could ignite the core-wood of ebony, and mine. I thought to invite her for dinner, but changed my mind. My intentions were almost honorable, but if she were seen with a pale stranger she might be branded as a prostitute. It would not be so bad in Quibdó—but I did not know her circumstances.

At Boringen I got a small, whole, deep-fried catfish, with opaque eyes staring at me without blinking. The fiery red rice was excellent, so while it was not sole meunière, it was satisfying. I was served by Boringen himself, and when he asked me about my day I lied, as usual, saying it was *"muy agreable, señor."* When I commented on the whiskers of the cat on my plate, he chuckled, the skin-fold under his chin flapping like the dewlap of a male iguana. I liked him, so while watching him, I became sad. I imagined he would die soon, because his protruding belly was stretched tight like a drum by venomous intestinal fat. I had a pint of golden brew, which tasted of the nectar of the Greek gods, and which I raised high, greeting, as usual, the passing-by citizens.

Back in my room I made myself a sweet Nescafe and retired to the balcony. I had already missed the sunset but the geckos were waiting for me, turning their eyes 180 degrees to watch my moves, frozen motionless, only to dash with the speed of light for the unsuspecting insect, and never miss. It started to rain with great might, creating a wall in front of my balcony, so the river disappeared. I felt as if hidden in a soft cocoon of privacy, alone with pleasantly unimportant thoughts.

When the hall-of-famer of world anthropology, Claude Levi-Strauss, wrote the famous *Tristes Tropique*, he certainly could not have known about the felicitous balcony, hanging, a little askew, above the mighty Rio Atrato with its occupant, screened from the whole world by the roaring water-wall of tropical deluge.

Fish and Snuff Chewing Venus

It has been observed that after a certain age many men stop asking questions and only speak, and later, after another certain age, they talk only about themselves. So when I asked D.J. questions he said he liked me, and said that I had to come to Houston. He asked me how old I thought he was. He looked about seventy, so when I said sixty-four he liked me even more, since he was seventy-seven. I expressed surprise to which he said only: Fish oil. Then smoothened his abundant salt-and-pepper hair demonstratively, opening his loosely hung jaw in a grin to display a snow-white upper denture. You have to come to Houston, he said, we'll go fishing, I know places.

We'll go to Galveston, he proposed. It ain't far, good road there, and on the way we might stop by those lowlands near La Marque or Alvin to get us some crabs. They make great bait—or soup, too, come to it.

You got some crab traps there? I asked.

He snickered and said, no traps, ma boy, we'll buy some chicken wings in Winn-Dixie, you tie a wing on string and lower it to the bottom of the canal, crab gets its pincer in it, you pull it out. Done. You have to come to Houston, I am telling you. We'll go fishing from my old pier there in

Galveston, there the fish come to you, not you to the fish, you'll see, we should have a time!

We took gulps of Bohemian Lager from San Jose in California, and put Gorgonzola on crackers. We did not talk for a while. It was September when we drank that Bohemian brew, when D.J. insisted again I had to come to Houston, but not until later in the year, since in September the water is too warm and the fish are in the deeps offshore.

They like to hang around the rigs there, in cold water, he said. Around Christmas is good. Then we'll have a very good time, I promise. We chased the beer with moonshine he brought from home, gulped it right from the jar.

I asked D.J., You must have some good fishing stories—and that question got him going, telling me what happened about a couple of weeks ago. I will tell his story now.

D.J. was fishing from his favorite pier in Galveston and that day he was lucky. He smiled happiness when he described his catch. First he got a small wahoo, under the limit, then two speckled trout. They call them sea trout in Florida but I like speckled, he said, since they have these colored dots all over, red and blue, on the shiniest silver torpedo, which changes to white gold when they come out, I swear to gods, you haven't seen a prettier creature in your life, I always kiss the trout. I do. One was a couple feet, good size, but the second one I got was even bigger, at least a ten-pounder. Specimen of wonder, my friend!

The sun was getting redder and bigger, sinking to the horizon of Gulf of Mexico by Matagorda, when a lady approached me, D.J said, she was an older negro woman. When he described her I thought he might be describing that favorite of archeologists, the famous Paleolithic clay Venus of Vestonice, with hips as wide as Texas, breasts a five-pounder each. The lady was black like midnight, D.J. said, and from that night her eyes, slanting a little, shined like brilliants, hundreds of carats, straight from Tiffany's, mon. Not yellow, yet.

The lady told him she had been watching. And what she saw was that none of the guys, on the long pier, didn't get nothin', no fish, not even a croaker, or drum, not even a grunt. And they were no nigger fishin', sir, they all have nice Shakespeare rods and on them the fancy Daiwa reels. And they used good bait, too, I saw those bad horse leeches (*Macrobdela decora*), them big night crawlers (*Lumbrius terrestris*), even live shrimp. I checked. But you sir, she said, but you, sir, you were the only one pulling them out, them trouts. So I checked carefully what you're doin' different. And what I see? I see you chew tobacco. So I said to myself, I'd ask the good gentleman for a chow, I figured, it could make the difference. She smiled her shy, pretty smile and D.J. flashed one back.

D.J. threw his hands in the air, did not know what to say so he said, Will do, reached into his tackle box, pulled out a tin of Copenhagen, and saying Good luck lady, it must do some good, he handed her the chewing snuff.

Thank you, thank you, sir, she said and like a real pro she packed the granular chow by snapping the tin with her wrist, opened the lid, took a pinch, put it under her very generous lower lip and smiled again a smile as wide as her hips. I am going, she said and marched to her fishing place, holding her rod high.

Well, what happened then, I asked. Did the snuff bring her any luck? I opened another bottle of the Bohemian Lager.

D.J said, you would not believe it. First I did not watch her, I was casting the new Rappala lure. Then all of a sudden I hear that high-pitched whine of a reel going crazy—and surely, it was hers, the chewing grandma. She loosened the break some, held the tip of her fishing rod up, I could see; she knew what she was doing. Exciting to see, believe me. The fish must have been big, it went straight, no diving, no zigzagging, frightfully fast, it had a purpose. Then suddenly the line went limp. I tell you, it hurt me to see it, hurt me right here. D.J pointed at his heart.

The woman pulled the line out of the water and on the hook was head of a catfish. The cat could have been of a good size, one can say only by the size of the head, cause the cat was cut at about pectoral fins. The woman brought it to me, with a sad face, and she just said "Shark, bastard." The head had Salvador Dali whickers, mouth from ear to ear with lips, and the beady eyes still alive.

But it was not a shark, the man in the gray suit, which did the surgery, D.J was sure. Judging from how the cut was smooth, surgical, as if cut by a belt saw, it must have been that killer torpedo, the gigantic barracuda, which sometimes comes to the shallows when the water gets cold. She might have been a scary five feet, or more.

Well, D.J. said, bad luck lady, it happens. Without much thinking he pulled his stringer from the water, unhooked the larger speckled trout, and handed it to her. The other one is plenty of fish for lonesome me, he told her.

One could not say if she blushed, but she took the trout without hesitation, thanked him simply, twice, and said the grandkids would be glad. Nobody else feeds them, you know how it goes, she told him. She took the cat's head, too, for a soup, you know. She spit the snuff into the water in the light chestnut-colored, smooth, powerful stream of a pro, and turned away. So, D.J. and Grandma were quite happy when they said goodbye.

I can say D.J. amused himself with the story. He shook his head and told me in a conspiratorial whisper, You have to come to Houston.

And me? Well, the lizard part of my brain, with Milan Kundera, told me that "Life is Elsewhere," so I am gonna go. To Houston.

Made in the USA
Columbia, SC
12 October 2018